I0680307

Polonio Pass

By Doc Krinberg

Aignos Publishing

Honolulu, Hawaii
2014

Published in the USA by Aignos Publishing, Inc.
1910 Ala Moana Blvd, #20A
Honolulu, HI 96815
www.aignos.com

Printed in the USA

Edited by Zachary Oliver
Cover design by Bryce Watanabe
Front cover photo used courtesy of Gregory LaBorde
Back cover photo used courtesy of Lieuwe Hofstra
Interior design by Liang Han Yu / Zachary M. Oliver

13-digit ISBN: 978-0-9895191-9-9
10-digit ISBN: 0-9895191-9-8

Aignos Publishing
Honolulu, Hawaii
2014

Dedication

For Laura
E Hoomau Maua Kealoha

Chapter One

Tom looked out the window, it was dusk and his reflection mirrored off the glass pane from the lamp's glow. He thought of that line in 'Moonlight Mile' about the face in the window...and knowing that face for so long. Behind and inside his face, the snow flurries blew to and fro. It would be dark in moments and then all he'd see was the bluish memory of the yard covered in snow...and the dark and his face.

Under the papers on his desk were the lab results, and all the technical hooey about the testing that he could give a rat's ass about now. The conversation with the oncologist and then his personal physician had pretty much laid it bare. So he stared at that familiar face in the window again. It took on the pallor of the snow outside.

The mail on top of the pile of papers held his early-bird RSVP for his 40th reunion in California at Revere High School. That familiar face in the window frowned at the invitation, one month until *that*. Seven or eight months until the big enchilada, casino, or sleep happened. Maybe. He thought of California. Brown hills in winter, chaos on wet rain-slicked streets from frantic drivers, cool air and the smell of wet dirt and...Raymond Chandler describing rain.... what the hell else did southern California smell like? He pulled the lab tests out from under the pile and after folding them, placed them in his pullout cabinet that locked; like porn, this was to be stashed away, only to be perused when alone and feeling like acting stupid.

He checked his face once more, the light from the front walk still letting him see some snow blowing and he decided to stay a little longer...in his mind, in California. Mary wasn't making dinner tonight as she was hanging with her cabala of art class pals, and he could afford to just get in the Way-Back Machine and think of Cali, and *her*, the other one. He reread the 40th reunion brochure and traveled to Nina. He didn't want to look in the window because that guy was old.

◯◯◯

"Are you sure you want to bother with that reunion? At the 30th one you sat with Corinne and just dished everyone up before you got sick from the dip they had," Art asked as he prepped some vegetables for a side dish, "and Corinne is someone I wouldn't hang with for any belated period of time. Her neck is fast giving Jabba some fucking competition. She'll be sitting there with a bucket of frogs this reunion."

Nina smiled at Art as she breaded the chicken. She always secretly enjoyed his tasteless jabs at old friends and relatives without allowing him the pleasure of knowing it. Art was relentless in skewering one or the other, holding them out in front of him like some speared, helpless reptile, until she'd finally make him stop with a jab of her eyes or just a simple *shut-up-Art-* smile.

Art despised Corinne, another friend from Nina's past who lived uncomfortably close in Los Angeles. Art had grown up, in what his son described as 'Rubeville' in the Midwest, and he couldn't wait to leave. The Marines had been his ticket out at seventeen. He didn't understand people who grew up in L. A., then moved four blocks from their parents. At least Nina moved away from her mother and father up the coast into a home that was a comfortable fifty minutes to the south.

"I wanna go to this one," Nina laughed," you *know* some chins and tummies will be in wheel barrows and some serious plastic work will be going on. It should be a scene and a half."

"Better wear a hard hat for some of the falling flesh, baby," he quipped, giving her a smile. It grew quiet as he finished cleaning up and placed the vegetables in the steamer pot. "Will Tom Kelleher be there?" He asked, breaking the silence.

She'd thought of Tom at the mention of his name, smiling inside. She'd tucked him away in the back of her mind for a long time, but Art was the one that opened the door. Not her. She shrugged, "I don't know." *Liar*. She'd seen him on the RSVP list online at the website for the reunion. *And* Face Book. She didn't mention it before, but she knew Art had seen him there, too. Rubes from Rubeville weren't so hot at covering their tracks or poker faces.

She hadn't seen Tom in almost thirty-five years, and yet, because of who he'd been...he still cast a very large shadow in her kitchen; almost the same size that Nina had cast in Mary's kitchen.

Chapter Two

Back when it started in the 1960's, Tom had black hair and wore it in the same DA ducktails with waterfalls, even when most of his friends were closer to Keith Richards in style. Tom's older brother, a beloved motor head that spent his early 60's in white tees that alternated in logos of *Bardhal* or Budweiser and grease stained jeans, even made the switch to denim bell bottoms, velvet shirts and wore his hair past his shoulders. But not Tom. He'd stayed consistent; sticking with his button fly Levis, snap button shirts, and boots or Converse canvass high tops. Nina was at times exasperated in trying to adorn him with something contemporary and dragged him to Fred Segal's and Century City to shop. Even with his lanky frame, fit for rock star clothing, he just never eased into new things she wanted him in. Off kilter, he'd twitch around in the tops as if burdened by a hair shirt, or complain that he was used to buttons and not zippers when he needed to piss.

So after the initial attempts, she finally gave up and allowed him his Zen. The inky Elvis-like haircut to the collar and faded Levis was him. She loved grabbing his hair in a bunch in her hands, fingers with black sprays sticking out in between and kidded him about his *luscious glory* when they did their *nad-sat* routine, substituting words to sound more intellectual. When they were fourteen, she'd just run her hands along his hair in a smoothing motion as they made-out in theaters or at parties. By high school, she craved pulling it and controlling it like different speeds on a shifter when they had discovered other things besides making out. He'd catch her looking at him and smiling, wondering what, and then she'd just take one of his Winston's and tell him how crappy they tasted.

He knew it was her way of covering her thoughts and let it happen. He always felt out of his depth with her. Knowing too much might be a dangerous thing. She was Mensa sharp, like a small lithe javelin, honed by her parents for big things and a big school. Tom was happy to be where he was and played like a mushroom in the dark; fed shit if it meant no rocking of the boat. But he truly did love her…there was no doubt in his mind that what he felt was genuine and solid. And he did so enjoy having her pull his hair.

◙◙◙

Sitting back now, not looking at his reflection anymore, Tom allowed himself to think of them both, wife and old flame. Mary had also used his hair as a speed shift when they first met. He reflected and smiled, letting himself drift in between the two women like a body swimming between two different boats in the water… admiring each for their unique lines and the cut of their respective sails. He'd do this when he was alone, thinking he wouldn't feel the pangs of guilt or remorse or loss for thinking of each of them together. Knowing neither knew what in hell he thought anyway, both at a loss of his personal, reflective thoughts of both women. As he floated between them, he still felt moored and secure, his wedding band acting as a sea anchor, preventing him from being dragged too far out into open waters and swifter currents...or slack, allowing him to surf small waves like a bobbin too close to Nina's memory. The round gold anchor on his left hand gave him security and a sense of snug.

He'd gaze at Nina and picture her at nineteen or twenty, and then he'd try, wishing to tell her, thinking in his head that she was a bookend in his life's novel. He'd marvel at thinking something like...that she was a support and a beginning to one side of his life, setting the trajectory for things to come. She was there in the beginning and had shaped him and filled him.

He'd never told her *ever,* how much of a foundation she'd given him. That in many ways, she was like a blind architect, envisioning what it was they wished to construct, yet even in this blindness, able to imagine different angles and understand a different math. She had given him, like this unseen vision and unknown structure, ideas and stories and music and art. Taking him to museums, reading aloud from literature he'd never heard before, playing guitar as he listened...lost.

In all this, she had no idea how she was creating him for the future. Not just for other women, but also as a man in many ways. She filled him with more than his father or mother had ever been able to...in the ways he was desirous to learn and be. In the way that her parents had worked so laboriously on creating *their* structure, she did for Tom. Yet she had no idea of the effect on him, other than when he'd pay rapt attention to her playing or read him an article or explained art. Tom always felt full when he left her, his head a whirling dervish of ideas and questions. He started collecting his own books, listening to different music. But it all had a seminal place in what he absorbed around Nina.

While he drifted in that channel of water in between the two, he'd wondered how he would've turned out having not known her. He'd been content in thinking himself smart, not really knowing more than any other guy who tinkered on motorcycles or helped his brother change the oil on his '55 Fairlane that he street raced. Even at fourteen, she could discuss the news and understand it, explain 'escalation' and what it meant for Tom when he turned eighteen and became draft eligible if he decided to finish high school, but forego college. And in her eyes, there was no other option than for him other than to finish high school and attend college. Despite her parent's reticence concerning Tom and her, Nina had this vision of the two of them attending school, growing old together, having the house, and the kids. Tom used to kid her about feeling like 'Gumby', her little green ball of clay that she was molding and fixing to fit her own tastes and desires.

She fretted when he became lost within himself, repairing an old bike he and his brother had saved from a junkyard or was lost in the crowd at Irwindale Raceways watching his brother race in heats for streetcars. She couldn't be a part of it. Couldn't see herself as one of those chicks wearing short-shorts with half their asses exposed, push up bras, and B-52 'doos'. She cursed this trailer park side of Tom and blamed his brother and dad for keeping him there. Black fingernails from motor oil, a rag sticking out of the back pocket, and a pack Winston's rolled up in his sleeve, always tinkering with his tools, and fast food or Mac n' Cheese for every meal.

The brothers were always working on their bikes and cars and listening to Link Wray like they were trapped in some black and white television episode of the late 50's. The boys she had attended grammar school with had pretty much developed along the same lines as their fathers: golf lessons, tennis, Europe in the summer at fifteen, and probably a new or almost new car at sixteen. Tom socialized with them all, yet was never really allowed total entry to their world. And, naturally, many even resented Nina's attraction to Tom when they started going steady at fourteen, feeling their entitlement threatened.

Tom smiled broadly, but didn't know what to do when he received a note from a girl named Naomi that he'd been friends with since 6th grade. In the note, she asked him if he liked Nina Hassel. There wasn't a boy in 8th grade that didn't know or like Nina Hassel. He had attended another elementary school and had noticed her since 7th grade after entering junior high. She was taller than most girls and had thick, rich, flaxen blonde hair thick, not wispy like some blondes were. In the summers she tanned darkly, not pale skinned and married to sunscreens or Coppertone. She wore very short skirts and usually tights, but on some days she didn't. And in US History, where Tom sat in front of her in the next aisle over, he'd sneak furtive peeks over his shoulder at her un-lady like style of sitting. Yes, he liked her. And when he answered Naomi's note in the affirmative he, like so many others, had serendipitously altered his life with a fluid decision.

Chapter Three

"Tom? I'm home. You there?"

Mary's return had him abruptly sit up as if he were still floating and took alarm at something underwater brushing against him. *Guilt?*

"In here."

She walked in. He focused on her outlined reflection in the doorway behind him, framed as if in a picture, smiling. "Readying some lecture? When you're in your *sanctum sanctorum* I know you're up to schoolwork. Is that sophomore class giving you more headaches?"

He swiveled around to face her. "I can only answer two or three questions at a time," he quipped smiling. "Actually," he said, telling a partial truth, "I was thinking of floating in the sea between two beautiful boats...then was taken by a shark."

"Nice." She strolled lightly to his chair and swiveled it so his back was to her and they could see each other's reflection in his window. After a pause, "Who are those people?"

"In the window, there's a face you know..." he said softly.

"Do I know you, Tom Kelleher?"

"Yes, I am the man who brings you roses…when you aint got none…"

She grabbed his white hair, "On the Stones again? 'Loving Cup'?"

He reached around from behind and grabbed her ass. "Always."

"Have you eaten?"

"No. I've been sorting mail and just hanging out. Floating, like I said."

"Did you hear from Will?" Will was an old friend since middle school that had broached the idea of attending the 40th reunion in the first place. Will had joked about what everyone would look like.

"I did. He joked about trying to get a facelift before the big event. He says his jowls are fast approaching Droopy-Dog reaches."

"Thankfully yours aren't. Who else is going to show, do you think?"

"I don't know, but there's an RSVP page and there's only about thirty-something people who bothered to even login." *And Nina had not. This would be typical of her*, he thought.

Tom glanced up at Mary. Her skin had fine lines as if rendered by an artist to convey a face that enjoyed smiling and saw little worry. Her forehead was almost smooth, and he always loved how her thick wavy hair framed it, her part on the side. When they met she had a plumeria flower behind her right ear. Her figure had changed little, as well. She never needed a brassiere, but wore them. Flowing among the dark waves of her hair were shiny slivers of silver, woven finely into the dark mesh, and could only be seen when she was in sunlight. Tom remembered smiling when they met, and when he was first cognizant of his feelings for her, besides sexual. In the window in front of him, she stood behind him, her torso and face above, hovering in the glass, now looking at him, now looking at herself, *thinking what?*

Mary gauged herself as much as Tom was remembering her back in the 70's. *Why hasn't he fucked me more,* she wondered. Does this reflection make him not want me, this woman in the glass? What's in this portrait I'm looking at that makes him turn away in bed, his back my only point of reference, if I had to identify his remains for the police?

He looked up at her, and she saw how his scalp had a light halo on the crown. Is he just too old now or is it I dried up and am not even caring for it anymore? She grabbed a clump of his hair and started twisting it back and forth, in the way the snow blew outside...fanning it one way and then the next. He was smiling now, as she did it, and started making car noises, shifting noises.

He teased her, "You haven't driven me lately...scared I'll stall?"

She shrugged playfully. "I don't know...been awhile since I've even seen your upholstery...is it still intact?"

"I think so. You look beautiful, Mary."

He meant it.

"Thank you," she whispered softly, cupping a hand under his chin and lifting his head as she bent to kiss him.

Her hair fell forward as she leaned over his face, and he found her lips inside the shroud of wavy, fragrant strands. He didn't mind the awkwardness of their mouths being in opposition, up and down, and reached to find the hem of her sweater blouse and ran his hands up to her bra. Under the material her small brown nipples were hard and familiar. He'd occasionally sneak glimpses of them when she brushed her teeth in the morning while wearing one of his tees or her tank tops for sleeping, or through the blur of the shower glass, visible even on her dark skin like the first time in Kapiolani Park. Now he squeezed them and her lips grabbed his harder. Their mouths opened at the same time, knowing each other was ready. How many times had they started kissing and performed the same dance of light kisses and then as if a timer went off, opened their mouths to take all of each other. Mary's lips were equal in thickness, and soft, so soft. He loved when during a kiss she'd smile into his mouth and then pull away her face, sweeping her hair back to survey the effect on him, and she did it now. His hands up under her top holding her tips, he started squeezing her breasts making the smile fade into biting her lips. He stole a quick gaze in his window to watch them, reflections mirrored in the glass, and felt the confines of his pants as he erected slowly. She sensed this and started to unbuckle his old leather belt and started pulling the buttons open on his fly, then started kissing him again. Her hand pulled him free of his shorts and she held him in her hand, thinking I'd know this prick. This is *my* prick.

Chapter Four

He walked back into the bedroom with two bottles of Corona, a ritual they had followed since their first night together. That first night in Hawaii in the 70's, he had watched her get out of the bed, sweating, her hair crazy and tangled, walking down the short, narrow hallway barefooted to the kitchen in her small one bedroom on Collins off of Montserrat, up against Diamond Head.

"No Primo?" He had asked, taking the beer, rubbing the cold glass on his forehead.

"I hate Primo. Don't support the local breweries. These taste better and I like limes." She took a drink and half the bottle disappeared. She smiled, her teeth dazzling in the half dark, "I like Coronas and *haole*-boys!" she said, then laughed loudly.

◯◯◯

"Come here, *haole* boy." She said in the dark of their bedroom. He handed her the beer. "Thank you…that was ver' nice…you still got that steel kine tongue, eh?" she kidded in pidgin.

He drank and said, "You're welcome, *wahine*. Pleasure be mine." He'd lost his erection somewhere in the middle and just let her push his white head down. He felt bad and didn't feel bad at the same time. He made her scream obscenities and that was a good thing. He didn't care if he hadn't come. He hadn't planned on this happening, far from it, but he was happy it did. This time no ED pills, so it was a crapshoot for him and he tried to hang as long as he could. Mary screaming naughtily was good enough for him, and his jaw still hurt from being in the vise of her strong thighs. Had it been that long that he didn't know she was shaved down smooth?

He drank the Corona easily. The bottle was sweating as much as he was. He hadn't really stood in front of her nude like this in a while…yea, toweling off after a shower if she walked in didn't count. Just standing, showing for her like this was something he always enjoyed. So he drank while she sat up against the pillows, one leg up.

"Why has it been so long?" she asked.

He rubbed the condensation sweat around with his thumb on the bottle, "I don't know. We asked that the last time. When did you shave?"

She laughed, "'Member? I mentioned it when I started swimming at the fitness center. Tried to talk you into going?"

He had balked trying not to let on how fatigued he felt, and had started his worrying and physician visits. "Right…well, I like it smooth like that, *wahine*."

"I couldn't hear you…come closer," she said, setting her empty bottle on the nightstand, "come here and tell me." She opened her arms and Tom drank the remains of his beer and crawled into bed next to his wife.

Chapter Five

Art listened to Nina breath in the dark. For years, he had studied her breathing as if he were an anthropologist in the throes of some experiment on sleeping patterns of indigenous Angelinos. She usually watched him fall asleep, a book in between her fingers, but frequently, he'd wake up in the dead of night and listen to her.

When Nina had her rough patches, and he listened raptly and protectively, he would man the rails all night if necessary. Back in those days, on and off, she downed different medications, and he paid strict attention to any anomalies in her homeostasis. And even though he'd been the keeper of the keys and the watcher at the gate, she would, at times, rebuke him or turn on him entirely; she rode small waves of medicinal delusions and problems occurred with the post-alcoholic yipps. Art hung through the thick of it and now in the dark felt relieved at how evenly she breathed. Her blonde hair, whiter in streaks, was still thick and looked silky. At times he'd touch it and enjoy the softness and actually be aroused because it was her hair. She still aroused him deeply.

She went through menopause, at times feeling like a cat in heat one moment and a wolverine the next. Twisting and turning from some inner heat she had no control over, fighting against the fine white hairs she found hiding on the underside of her jaw line near her chin. *Jesus,* she thought, *am I going to be fucking Mammy Yoakum?* She took care of that situation promptly. Religiously, she'd place a pencil under her tits to see what sort of grip she had and remembered a time when she and Tom laughed at older women at Venice Beach who had drooping tits, and he'd repeat Brando's line from *Tango,* concerning playing soccer with them as they aged.

Sometimes, Art would gently touch her as she slept. He'd touch under her sleeping tees and savor the feeling of her skin. To his fingers, it was a priceless discovery each time. But he had trouble simply saying it, breaking it down into terms that didn't sound corny or lame…have her think him an imbecile! He wondered what it'd be like to never have this side of the bed filled with her; stray hairs, afterlife of her perfume, shampoo smell embedded in her pillow, the hidden candy wrappers stuffed in between sheet and cover…he couldn't think of it. In his case, he felt that had he left her, there'd be no trace of himself left, as if a large wave washed up where he had stepped onto the beach and pulled all traces of his existence back into the sea.

Art lived for her. In the blueness of the unlit room, he made out her outline in the crumpled, white sheet. The dip of her midriff from the hip, a place he enjoyed running his hand as she dreamed. Did she know what *he* looked like when asleep? Did she listen to *his* breathing?

One solitary tear ran down his cheek as he turned over and let himself fade out.

Chapter Six

Art watched the weather channel as he tied his tie. Snow flurries and brutal wind chills there in the east. He looked out the window, the climbing late March sun just touching the oleanders in the yard. He liked this time of the morning, the stillness of the house when it was settled from the night as if it too had a restful sleep and lay languidly in its own bed, satisfied. He could smell the wood furniture when he wasn't moving, the house endowed with cooking smells, walking past it, taking it for granted. When he was single, in the years before Nina, he lived in a small wooden house behind a main house off Wonderland in Laurel Canyon with cedar walls and oak and maple furniture. He smoked there and took that house for granted, too. But in the early dawn, when he sat on the lanai and drank coffee before the traffic monster awoke, he could smell his wooden house; a rich humidor of masculine scents. He sat down now in a carved, mesquite rocker that he'd bought in Texas for a drier time in his life and realized it was one of two survivors from those bachelor days. The other being his footlocker/cruise box stashed in the garage that he'd kept from his stint in the Marines, the rest of his treasure from that life, now just driftwood and flotsam in the past's wake.

He meditated on this and just let himself drift back out in his memory. Nina, when he first met her, and how he had felt something catch inside. He'd been married before and had children but nothing prompted him for how she affected him when he saw her.

He was done with his first wife and living in the Laurel Canyon cabin. He drove a 'beater', 57 Porsche Speedster that showed bondo patches from bow to stern. The alimony and lawyer fees from years ago had a lasting effect on him. The cabin he rented was behind a main property built on a forty-five foot hill, practically needing a 4-wheel-drive jeep to make it up his part of the road that looped behind the main house. A doctor in Laguna, who rented it to musicians, owned the entire property, but the old Porsche did nicely digging it out in 2nd gear. In his previous life, he would've been throwing rocks at the house in front, but now as he settled back into single life, he found himself wishing they'd played louder. So he'd sit on the lanai with a cigarette and a beer, his tie loosened, and just decompressed. Giving up on the 'monk' thing he had going on and feeling like Fred Mertz, he shaved his head as baldness became the new thing. He started to reenter that area of knowing more things about himself that somehow had been shuffled out, or bagged and tagged, and placed in the attic of forgotten men.

He had wrapped himself around the axle of work, taking his eyes off the ball while somebody else replaced him quietly in bed and out. He vowed to never allow that to happen again, determined to stay true to who he was and somehow balance it out, if and when he got involved again. With Nina, he'd struck a balance, if not a deal of sorts.

As she held sway over the decorations of their abodes, he was allowed his eccentricities and objects de art he found fanciful; yet over time, he relinquished his grip on the past as she shared it with the Goodwill and Salvation Army folk; bit by bit. What had been quite the collection of himself, had gradually been whittled down to the mesquite rocker that had been explained to him about its prowess in hotter and drier climes, and his Gila like grip on his footlocker, filled with Marines' stuff.

When did he start softening on the deal, he wondered…*how did so much of him go out the door and into a truck bound for strangers*? Smiling, he put it up to Nina's resolve and inner patience. On the surface, she was in a hurry and impatient mode, yet inside she had the constitution of a Galapagos tortoise. She had merely waited him out, and like a weathered stone revealing its true inner workings, she packed and parceled most of his past away and lay claim on her domain. The rocker, the only visible piece of the life he had above water now, the rest had been swept away by an unrelenting tide of her tastes and needs.

He finished his coffee, rinsed the cup, and placed it in the sink. Nina slept still; he left the house as quietly as he could.

Chapter Seven

Mary's dad was from Papua New Guinea and her mom was mixed Hawaiian who reflected about every race that had stepped foot on Oahu. She was what the locals termed a *poi dog*. As a teen, she had posed for different local magazines, usually in a Mother Hubbard or muumuu with a hibiscus poised behind her ear to designate 'old times' for advertisers. One photographer described her as a 'Gauguin girl', so that helped her to get extra work.

When Tom first saw Mary, his first thought was she was like that painting of Gauguin that Nina and him saw at an exhibition in Los Angeles for a birthday gift years ago. He was on a kick to flee to Tahiti then, and live some idyllic silliness that Nina dismissed in what she termed as 'latent runaway syndrome.' He laughed at her description because, in essence, it was true. He just wanted to run away for a bit and not answer to anything or anyone. But as usual, Nina had introduced him to another artist that he fell in love with. She seemed to know what would excite him, stir him inside, and fill him with pleasure.

When he saw Mary that first time, the door swung open to his mind, to that day at the L.A. museum, giving him a brief glimpse of Nina, but he hurriedly shut the door on that vision as abruptly as a wind-shut slamming urging him to concentrate on Mary. He had been in the islands for a week, the ship he was sailing, a container vessel, was outbound for Guam in three more days, and he stood his watches and had time off. It was his second ship after two-and-half years of sailing. He'd been down in Waikiki, at the International Marketplace checking out the tons of island schlock when his boredom took him walking. He was in Kapiolani Park, walking along the promenade and beach walk when she breezed by him with a surfboard tucked under her arm, her black bikini top punctuated by her small, hard nipples, and he thought of the woman holding the melon in "Two Tahitian Women."

Her thick pulled-back hair was wet, in parts, reflecting the sun. Yet, she stopped and placed a fallen plumeria blossom behind her ear, her arm holding the board muscled and toned. They exchanged glances. He expected the usual expression of facial disdain he received from local girls accompanied by the pidgin words *bodda you?* Basically meaning, *what's your problem?* But he was surprised when she smiled quickly and greeted him with the more jovial *howzit?*

It was mandatory for him to take a second look at her ass after she passed by. A southern guy who worked in engineering called them 'onions' and all he could think was, *what a nice onion.* Hard and rounded in her board shorts, he fell in instant lust with her. That she looked again, her white smile and a quick flash stopped him dead in his tracks. Then he went to the sea wall and sat, watching her stroll easily down until she came to one of the park's outdoor showers. She set her board down, stepped under it, and pulled the chain to rinse off.

So he sauntered back easily, trying his hardest not to look hurried and crazy. She knew he'd follow her and liked how he looked. He was totally non-local, but also didn't look like the usual corn-fed vacationers she encountered on a daily basis. He was different, in that he didn't wear a loud aloha shirt or shorts exposing white legs, but instead had a faded tee shirt with a Triumph motorcycle logo and faded Levis. His hair was coiffed in what she called then a, 'loose McGarrett'...his black hair in a falling pompadour. He was tall and lean but muscled, and she liked that, wondering if he surfed. He strode back to her and sat on the wall opposite the shower near the old natatorium, watched her rinse her hair, bend over, and show her back to him, broad shouldered with almost manly abs tapering to a thin waist.

When she stood back up and turned, shaking the water from her face, he quickly turned away to check out at the surfers off Diamond Head. She knew he wanted her to see him looking, yet be nonchalant as well. Finally, she gave her board a quick rinse and went over to the wall and sat down beside him. She shook her head like a dog that had just galloped in from the rain, pelting him with droplets as the tips of her hair raked his shoulders.

"Is this where you apologize and take me home to dry me off?" he asked.

She threw her head back and laughed, "I hadn't thought of that..."

They met later at the Rainbow Hilton bar and swapped stories and drank mai tais. Her hair was swept back and she had a plumeria behind her ear again. She wasn't surprised he was a sailor, but frowned at the fact he was leaving so soon. He made her laugh and he held his booze pretty well, and wasn't falling over her, trying to play with her hair like most men. She hated that, having a hand take her hair up or have it stroked. Even local *kine* guys would act stupid that way. She preferred haole men, but also cringed when they started out talking about island girl fantasies or worse. She had dated a French guy once who was attending UH before she met Tom, and he'd rage about Polynesian women when he drank, wanting to drag her to Tahiti to live in a yurt on the beach. She quickly extracted herself from that one.

"You're not going to ask me to run away to Tahiti with you?" She questioned as they walked along the water after their drinks.

"Actually I was thinking of Ricky Nelson's *Travelin' Man* and the line about Waikiki."

She laughed, "That's wrong on so many levels, Tom."

"Being honest and attempting to say worse things, I can." He joked.

Their tracks stopped on the beach. He wanted to freeze frame her, take a snapshot he'd be able to think about later, capture that one moment in the night that would be *the* memory. He knew he was leaving; that couldn't be stopped, and he also knew that whatever fun he had tonight was over. So he wished to take a mental token with him.

There were no plans to stop in Honolulu on the way back, as the crew left the containers and took back others for the mainland US.

He was a machinists mate apprentice, and at the bottom of the maritime food chain. He described his serfdom as they drank, not embellishing it.

He couldn't help but to hold Mary against Nina, who had taken up so much of his life. They were so opposite that he had to question himself whether that was part of the attraction…and he truthfully realized that it was. Even Mary's darkness and her clichéd exoticness were a polar difference and her athleticism and natural ease in clothing. When they met at the bar, she had on old faded jeans, slippers, and a aloha shirt of vintage quality. Her hair was casually pulled back to one side to allow her magenta and white plumeria blossom to show brilliantly contrasting its dark nest, a beautifully crafted egg. He remembered the first one she wore was yellow and white, this blossom now far more beautiful in the night air as he looked at her.

"You changed your flower"

She smiled." You noticed. Different kine color…even smells different to me."

He leaned in towards her ear to smell it, aware that people were walking by and that many were out walking the beach, laughing and talking. But he inhaled the soft and delicate petals of the flower, lost in the fragrant smell of her hair. He couldn't untangle the two, so enjoyed them equally. Mary brought a hand up to his neck and turned him slightly with her fingertips. She kissed him. He was surprised, it was unexpected, having bookmarked that memory of her standing there; the lights of the city on part of her, a chiaroscuro beauty to take back to sea. Her kiss was soft and firm and he let himself melt into her as they pulled closer.

He didn't remember how they got back to her small flat in a row of apartments built in the late 50's. But when back out at sea, he reflected many times on drinking Coronas in her place and eating take-out Chinese. Amazed, she had also watched him throw out his cigarettes when she voiced her distaste for kissing smokers.

She looked at his address and sat drinking a beer that was the last remaining from the final six-pack of his stay, before she drove him back to Sand Island where his ship was berthed. He explained about the ship as they drove, but she wasn't really listening. He didn't know how to handle this separation since he had only separated from Nina under duress. She had revealed her relationship with a guy she worked with, so he just kept talking. She finally told him to shut up. She parked and pulled him to her and they kissed. Just kissed. He seemed to sense that this kiss wasn't just any other kiss. It was a long kiss, meant to be remembered, not taken lightly. She kissed him with all of her, engulfing him, trying to let her pent up spirit loose inside of him. She didn't believe in much of the things her Papua granny put a lot of stock in spiritually and South Pacific kine thoughts, and though she never took pork with her over the Pali, which was obvious bad luck, she knew she wanted to have him take some measure of her with him, inside his heart and mind.

And, he did.

She started writing him letters that night. In the stolen Triumph tee she wore as her new nightshirt. She started, "Aloha, haole-boy…"

Chapter Eight

They attended a James Dean double feature at the Nuart. Supposedly, Vampira, who claimed she had slept with Dean and talked to him in the spirit world, would be there, but she was a no-show. Tom was let down since he'd looked so forward to it.

"Man, seeing her would have been cool."

Nina shook her head, "You just wanted to see her tits," she quipped, giving him the fish-eye.

"Nothing wrong with that...it's healthy and they're damn huge," he laughed. They had rode up to the theater on Tom's Thunderbird, so both were in jeans and leathers, and Nina felt they looked so very cool. She was very cognizant of people staring at her and what she had on from an early age. Her face had set her apart from other children in her odd mix of Scandinavian and Asiatic genetics. Her mother was Russian and reflected a lot of Tartar blood. In Nina, the mix gave her northern Europe's coloring and almond shaped, light eyes that shifted between blue and gray with a turned down Bardot mouth. With her hair falling outside her black worn leather jacket, the contrast was eye catching and she enjoyed the looks from both men and women. She knew what the men thought, yet also wondered what the women thought, how they viewed her, and also how they viewed Tom as well. As they mulled around in the lobby getting popcorn, she enjoyed the attention. Tom was oblivious to her thoughts, and inside she liked that as it gave her more line in which to run and think different things, wonder about others. They entered the movies and suffered through the coming attractions.

Tom leaned over, "If we see *Citizen Kane* again I'll be blowing up Xanadu or Sloppy Joe's..."

She shushed him and he teased, "When will they have, *Fistful of Dollars* again?" She giggled when he shifted into his *such a guy* mode to make her laugh. He straddled so many different things and she liked him for that. Even though his love of bikes and all things with tools and grease wasn't particularly exciting to her, she loved the end result and sitting on the back of his bike, his hair dovetailing in front of her with the wind and the sheer energy of feeling it as he tore around corners or they went out into the sunlight of PCH, unbound for huge stretches of coastline and few traffic signals. Then there was the side of him she nourished and took to heart almost as a mission. Arts, literature, film...gossip or utter trivial nonsense that he paid rapt attention to because of the sender; himself an open, yet biased receiver. She also found in him a raw poet who threw some lines together ignorant of quatrains but primitive in expressing sight and feelings. He shared these with only her, embarrassed by this discovery in some ways and in private allowing himself to garner her attention and review.

It was the fifteenth anniversary of Dean's death in central

California making the double feature more potent in its showing. The soaring scores in *Eden* and the brother versus brother theme didn't really grab Tom as much as it did Nina. She hugged him harder when Cal and Abra were alight on the Ferris wheel and they shared that first pure kiss, finally admitting they were in love with each other. And after the scene, she pulled him to her and replicated the kiss. Tom came alive when Cal punched Aaron, grabbing her arm, almost throwing his own punch with the other hand.

They went outside for a smoke after the movie and while Tom looked for Vampira, Nina gazed at Tom. She pictured them growing old together and wondered what that would be like. *It can't be like it is between my parents,* she thought, *I won't go there.* She eschewed any hippie lifestyle either. Not shaving my legs, eating out of a communal pot, squatting somewhere to pee...no way baby! She knew that as much as she enjoyed some of the fashion and liked her suede Native American jacket like Neil Young's, that's where it ended. The movie, Cal and Abra piqued her curiosity at intermission. What happened to them? Did they care for Cal's dad until he passed? Did they have their own children? She hated when movies or books left that open question of where people went and what they did just as much as she feared in a way her own future ... and if Tom were really going to be a piece of her future. She looked at him, and he caught her glance and smiled back and leaned down to kiss her neck, her ear.

"What's up?' He asked.

"Nuth-in'...", she drawled, slyly.

They went back in for *Rebel* and Tom was much more into this feature. The Los Angeles locales, the fact that Jim Stark was an outsider and had to hassle with people was closer to home. For Nina, she was still tethered to *East of Eden* and thought about the entire novel and most of all of Lee, the Chinese houseboy who basically raised Cal and Aaron. She thought of her own father, so distant, the Depression era upbringing and his stoicism, wanting to be like him in many ways and also just wanting a kiss or a kind word instead of inquiries to grades or upcoming school events he'd have to take time out for. What sort of dad would Tom be? He was fun to be with, would his children see that too…or is that the fun only meant for lovers? Where was the switch, the difference? And what of *timshel*, the Hebrew word Lee spoke to end the novel? The word meaning, *"thou mayest rule over it."*

What was it she wished to rule over?

The entire movie was pretty much a blur for her and then it was over and Tom started doing Dean impressions on the way back to where they'd parked his bike. She pulled her hair back into a ponytail as he turned on the gas petcock and started kicking the bike over. He pulled his goggles out of his jacket, gunning the bike, and she put on her shades as he sat down and she straddled the machine.

"Coast Highway?" She yelled over the engine.

He rocked the bike side to side to feel the gas in the tank, then satisfied yelled, "You got it." He nodded, smiling back. They rode down to the coast and jumped on PCH at Santa Monica Pier and turned north under the signs that said 1 North and flew down the hill.

On these runs, Tom would open up the bike wide open in some

stretches and usually ran out towards Malibu or Trancas. Both lost in their own thoughts, punctuated only by her squeezing him with her thighs to remind him she was there, or his reaching a hand back and grabbing what he could. The bike was always sexual for her. The constant hammering of the twin exhaust pipes on each side, the acceleration at his fingertips, being only inches from the pavement all seemed to flow into her body. She had never felt so alive than sitting on Tom's bike. Sometimes, she'd reach down from his waist and feel him up; he'd respond, and she liked the power over him, overcoming his concentration on the machine. She felt that Abra had that power over Cal without him realizing it. The feeling made her warm inside.

In Malibu he stopped at a small coffee shop for late night coast drivers that had a mix of artists, bikers, and tired families needing a bite or some caffeine. When they pulled up, it was almost deserted.

"Where is Rod Serling and his prolific prologue? This place looks creepy tonight," she laughed.

They took time to wipe their eyes and noses from the ride. The coastal air was wetter than in the city. Nina pulled out her pony and started to brush out her hair as Tom turned away to pinch one nostril blowing through the other. She turned away, disgusted when he did that, and chalked it up as a *guyism*. They entered the coffee shop, both separating to enter their respective restrooms, and then found a table. The wind from the bike had swept Tom's hair into a huge pushed back wall of hair, duck tailed naturally by a 60 mph wind, and seeing him this way made Nina desire him, still aroused by the long ride up the coast.

"We should plan a get-away at one of these old motels out here on the way up to Santa Barbara and spend a night," she told him over the menu.

He smiled. "That'd be nice, maybe all the way to Santa Barbara since it's only 90 miles up the coast. But there're also a lot of places in Oxnard."

She nixed that stating that it was Tijuana-North in Oxnard. "What would you tell your parents?"

"Hmmm…that I was planning on fucking you after a long motorcycle ride and the side of the road is too rough."

"Yea, that will fly." They laughed together.

They smoked, waiting for coffee and pie. "He was killed up north of here, Jimmy Dean."

He nodded, "On the way to a race. In his little silver Spyder."

"Yea. Up to Salinas, where they shot *East of Eden*. It was in a place called Cholame and the Polonio Pass."

"Really? Is it spelled like it or just rhymes with the Hebrew *shalom*?"

"Rhymes. Funny isn't it. Like 'aloha' it means hello and goodbye. We should go there and see where he died."

Tom liked that idea. "Definitely! Is it a bike or car trip?" He had no clue how far Cholame was, thinking it was closer to Salinas than Los Angeles.

She thought a bit. "Probably a car trip and probably an overnighter. It's up over the Grapevine off of Interstate 5."

"Could we get there by the coast?"

"I don't know…but don't you want to drive over his route and then come up to where he was killed, like in his footsteps…or tiretracks?" To Nina that made more sense than back dooring it, knowing Tom was looking for an angle to take the bike instead of driving up and then down the Grapevine.

"I guess." They finished their coffee and pie and smoked again.

"Do you think we're any different than our parents?" Nina asked him.

He curled his lips, "I hope so! Do you think they ever did shit like we do? I know for a fact your dad's never been on a bike, and your mom just doesn't seem the type to jump on." Then he stood and started pinching his pockets, looking for tip change and the bike key in the very same way her father did before a family drive, probing for his keys, change and cigarettes. Nina had to smile at the irony of his remark, its meaning totally lost on him.

Where the ride up to the coffee shop had her head buzzing and her desires up, the ride back was her just hugging him, head nestled into his back out of the main wind and almost sleeping.

Tom thought of Cholame and how it must feel to just explode when someone hits you like that. He remembered Buzz in *Rebel* just exploding like the universe in the scene in the Planetarium as his car hit the beach after the fateful chicken run. Bad luck.

When he dropped her off late, he set the bike in neutral and killed the engine, coasting up towards her garage on the side street behind the house. There they'd talk in whispers and kiss. Then she'd grab the top of his head, shift him around, and he knew that was 'goodnight' as she smiled back at him as she went through the fence to the backdoor. He'd turn the bike and let it coast down the hill, starting it only when he was a good half block away.

He wondered if it would be lame to try and find a red jacket like Dean's, decided it would be and enjoyed his ride back home.

Chapter Nine

They spent night upon night watching old TV and making jokes up about the early 60's kids' shows in the A.M. they had suffered thru before school or when sick; Sheriff John, Chuckles the Clown, Bozo, Skipper Frank, Tom Hatton, and Hobo Kelly. They would reinvent obscene lyrics to the originals and just laugh until their stomachs hurt.

The classics were on only sporadically, and late, and chopped to edited bits to make room for late night car commercials. But they hung out for them; seeing *Touch of Evil* clipped to a 90-minute version or tune into the late night creep shows to see Rondo Hatton and Bela Lugosi movies. Tom did impersonations of Rondo Hatton or an overly dramatic Lionel Atwill and made her sides split. Or, they would listen to records. Her LP collection was much better than his, as his brother and he pretty much wore a hole in *Aftermath* or the Link Wray albums they had since the late 50's and early 60's. Their copy of *Highway 61 Revisited* just scratched endlessly. Those nights were running out.

They were out of high school and both in first years at college. Tom was attending Santa Monica City College and she at UCLA. He didn't have the grades or SAT scores, and she told him it was cool as even James Dean attended SMCC before he transferred to UCLA. He was becoming a fixture at the house, spending weekends and other nights, her parents acquiescing and looking at him as the potential son-in-law now. Her father was extremely pained when he would drive up and see the motorcycle parked downwind of the garage. There was a friction that wasn't overtly obvious in the atmosphere, yet was increasing in heat. Nina's room was at the far end of the house now, since taking over the attic above the garage, so at least there wasn't any undignified meetings between father and suitor, both making for the bathroom at the same time. Yet, the sleeping arrangements were reaching a head and Nina's mother was becoming more and more an advocate of Nina's independence, not only from her home but also from Tom. Nina leaving and perhaps going to an out of state school would be a good thing and slowly started pursuing that end.

On the other end, Tom found himself spending more time at their house than his own, getting the opposite reaction from a father who wished he could've had Tom's freedom and luck and vicariously enjoyed his being at Nina's so much. He liked Nina, yet didn't know her as well he should, and realized he didn't know anyone really as well he should, most especially Tom. Tom's brother missed their joint working on bikes and racing the Fairlane. And, of course, Tom was a good helper and he didn't have to pay him with exception of cigarettes. Tom would pop in and out grabbing laundry or a bite to eat then rush back to Nina's as his need to be with her, this inchoate need he couldn't explain to himself, just left him at a loss if they were apart. One side of him whispered, 'not good' while the other said 'don't worry.'

Nina's mother never stopped being charitable or graceful with Tom nor did she stop her campaign of making Nina take a break from him. She did have a fondness for Tom as she recognized his love for Nina was absolute, but at their age it was becoming stifling and the two were smothering each other.

There came a break when the quarterly grades were administered and Nina's were suffering and it was obvious Tom was barely attending his classes, hanging out at UCLA to meet Nina in between classes and missing school meant the draft. Her parents were decidedly unhappy and sat her down. The camel's back, while not broken, was stressed to the snapping point and they put the brakes on the relationship. She was tearful, yet understood completely and while her feelings for Tom were unabated, she did see their point and they only said in words what she had been feeling inside since school started. Many men were also interested in her as well and she liked the added attention. A couple of them, her professors, and she was flattered that an older man gave her attention sexually. How to broach the new plan to Tom would be hard and there'd be an argument probably and some tears, but she felt that she could carry it off. She'd started feeling smothered herself and needed a break. They were also becoming more like sister and brother, in that even as close as they had become and were sleeping together regularly, they'd stopped making love. As they did before when living apart and it was something they had to grab and do for each other; a need so intense they'd immolate in each instance in some way, shaking at the intensity, and now he rolled over and she allowed him to do so.

She wondered, *Was this marriage*?

Tom never knew about the senior she met for coffee and ended up fucking in his car, then in his dorm room many times after. She didn't know about the Asian girl in his Humanities class who asked him for a ride declaring that she wasn't allowed to ride on motorcycles or even talk to white boys. As Nina widened the gap between them, he went to classes more and started wondering what he'd do without her, as it seemed they were going down that path. He felt his inner self was crumbling and he needed instances, like the girl in Humanities, to fill in that emptiness. It was simple; supply and demand. His supply of Nina was being tapped out and his demand of self-respect and manliness as he deemed it, needed supply. On the nights they did stay together above the garage, they'd both roll over in silent guilt from their affairs.

For Nina, it was very different as Tom had been her only lover, so she took in as much as she could, exploring successive lovers and comparing them to Tom. For Tom, it was more or less what his brother called 'holes and heartbeat' and don't see them again.

Nina then met Averill, who owned a gallery in Santa Monica, when she and her mother went to see some paintings that her mother wished to purchase. Averill was in his early 40's and meeting Nina, chatted her up and enjoyed the fact that she knew so much about art history and modern paintings. When her mom was looking at some sculptor, he gave Nina a card with his home number and asked her to call anytime. Within a week they had met, dined on Restaurant Row and slept together. He drove a Morgan and she liked the cozy interior, her leg right against the column where the gears were and the huge fur lined strap across the hood. She also liked the attention, his sophistication, and having lived in Europe, and while he did talk about himself a lot, she just chalked it up to older men impressing a younger woman. Nina was fast becoming invisible in Tom's life, and he called her on it one night when he came over.

"You can't stay tonight, Tom," she said, matter-of-factly.

"I hadn't counted on it, Nina," he answered lamely, hurt and not wishing it to show.

"I don't think you should drop by anymore either. Or at least call first." Her tone sent shivers and electrical signals in and out of his brain. He knew and didn't know. He wanted to say it, but just didn't have the mechanism in his tongue to do so.

She heard the hurt and confusion, yet in another way, she enjoyed the freedom and power she had over him now. It didn't matter that she loved him still; this was different. She told herself that she'd always love him, but she couldn't be with him now. She looked at him; the long sleeved snap button shirt, Levis, Chippewa boots, and Ray-bans. She held him up to Averill in his European clothes and tailored suits and wrap-around sunglasses. Maybe one day Tom would be like that, but he wasn't. He was the past.

"You're seeing someone else aren't you?" He stammered out.

"Yes. I am and I have been with a few other men as well," she glanced down avoiding his hurt. She couldn't take that look of his. Telling him was one thing; looking at him was quite another. She had too much of herself invested in him to take on his hurt. Better to cut the rope, even if he was swinging on it.

The 'fuck you' he hurled at her stung like a snap of his hand across her face. She watched him kick over the bike unsuccessfully. Twice. He refused to turn and show his tears. Mercifully, he started his bike on the third kick and flew off fishtailing down the road. She wondered if that vision were the last way she'd ever see him.

His anger didn't abate for a long time. Part of it was the sting of her words and picturing her in bed with other men. That was almost too much to bear, seeing her in different positions with strangers. The other part he couldn't take was the fact that she had the guts to come clean and tell him honestly how she felt. He was unable to utter one syllable of his own indiscretions. He'd been with Anna, the Asian girl, just the night before and with the girl from the Triumph dealership in Culver City. *Fuck it. Let her think you're the most virtuous cat in the world. Let her have that thought*, he rationalized.

Chapter Ten

Mary enjoyed the mail she received from him once they made landfall in Guam. She hadn't expected it, but when he arrived there were a few letters from her that were airmailed that made the port-mailing center. Guam wasn't so far from Hawaii that it'd take forever to get there. The planes they saw flying overhead from the ship, the jet streams going east held his mail in some instances. He was happy to see them.

He thought of her a lot on this leg of the journey. He took a tetralogy by Mishima to read for the passage and was well into the fourth book, *The Decay of the Angel,* by the time they pulled into Guam. He noted ironically that these were books Nina had recommended years ago when last they met, when he became a merchant seaman as a deckhand. He enjoyed them immensely and looked forward to finishing them.

Seeing the letters cheered him up. One from his brother that was filled with abundant *fuck yous* and a sign off note from his dad, the only letter he ever received in his life from them, to the newer ones on special stationery from Mary. He stared at the Hawaiian address. He'd written her probably ten letters and tore up eight before settling on two that neither committed him, nor exaggerated how he felt inside. He dropped those in the mail chute before collecting his letters onboard ship, when the yeoman/personnel guy passed them out. He held her letters close to him and didn't open them until after his first watch so he could shower and relax in his rack and read them leisurely.

Her letters created a huge light inside him as he read. He hadn't been this excited since reading Nina's letters the summer she had gone off to France with her family and received the *Aeropostales* and spun around like a top, a fifteen-year-old idiot. They were gone a month and he was empty without her. And Mary's missives held the same power. He wondered at that…how someone totally different could excite him the same way. It wasn't just the sex they had, or the moment on the beach as they walked and talked, it was more. She filled within him some deep void that had set in since he had quit Nina. He was having problems when the ship left Alameda enroute to Hawaii to receive more containers, that he couldn't stop thinking of Nina and things that perhaps he should have done differently. That was a wash, as each time he did he felt miserable. After he became a seaman, she had long since dropped out of UCLA, gone to work for a small independent studio as a script editor, they had failed at becoming a couple again and met a man who proposed to her. Just coming to grips with all that bothered him and made him sick inside. On his first time out, he had thrown up off the fantail of the ship, his other mates just putting it down to rookie seamanship.

Now, with Mary's letters undressed as they were in his rack

onboard, he was comfortable in avoiding any thought of Nina, the same way he had slammed the door on her memory when he thought of Gauguin's paintings when first looking at Mary. *Just lock and bolt that door, man*, he thought to himself. *It isn't healthy going in there anymore.*

Mary's letters started out always kidding around, calling him her pet name of 'haole-boy' and laughing at his farm boy tan when she pulled his shirt over his head that first night in her flat. Then she would break into her day-to-day business and make fun of people at work and at school. She just started as a senior at UH and was going to get her teaching certificate soon. He looked around the crew's mess where he was berthed and felt inadequate. Teaching certificate…how honorable. Sharing a room with the radio operator…not so much. He continued reading where she would hit a point, and he'd transcribe the transition into more intimate thoughts. It were as if he could see she felt comfortable in sundry items and then segue into 'him and her' stuff. She talked about him and her memory of his kisses and how he held her. She was 5'9" and muscular and many guys were put off by her stature, yet with him she felt almost dainty and small. She wanted to somehow tell him how important that was for her, and how it made her feel, so she would couch it in how he had made her feel like a woman, and not that he had melted her into him and so glad he hadn't made some remarks as to her physique. She admitted playing with herself as she thought of him and hoped he did too, with a 'wink-wink' to make it more humorous and not too intimate, like she was going to anyway, using him as a mental toy to reach her end. She hadn't worried because every night since Hawaii he had thought of her when alone in his rack.

His letters to her mirrored almost to the style what they were experiencing. The humdrum day-to-day routines, his watches, the small crew and whom he liked and disliked, and then he too would slip into revelry about their lovemaking and how she had made him feel. He hadn't given a thought to her being bigger than Nina, just accepted her as she was and didn't mince words. He was in love again and he felt good.

After making landfall, he called her twice, the first time she wasn't at home. Then he got her and they talked over each other, as there was a delay in the overseas connection. He felt like jumping ship in Guam, thought better of the consequences, and so rode it back to Alameda. Before he hung up the second time when they finally connected, he had asked her if she would mind if he moved out to Hawaii and she said, surprised at herself, no, she wouldn't mind in the least.

After he hung up, she wondered where he planned to stay. She decided for his own good it would be with her. Non-local white boy stumbling around only meant trouble in paradise. Mary would take care of that.

Chapter Eleven

Mary thought about that time as he slept in her arms, having finished their beers, and calling him back to her open arms in bed. She hadn't had an orgasm like that in a while, and she wanted to think about it. She felt his breathing and held him slightly easier to allow him to have some space. How do they grow apart so readily and get so wrapped up in minutiae? Forget this place, this beach they used to lay out on, and just make love when they felt it? That beach in their minds that was always in Hawaii…her small and closed in place they first made love in, and then the multiple living places after Tom went back to school and she was teaching. Then permanent on the mainland as they both grabbed jobs in the same city, yet in their minds always in Hawaii.

She thought of his upcoming reunion and what that was all about. He usually laughed them off with a 'who wants to see those assholes anyway?' Yet now he wished to go. He was curious as to what people looked like even though half were on Face Book. He said he knew those pics were old and they were faking it. He was proud of the fact that when he sat down he could still as he said it, see his tackle. She had run through his e-mail and had not seen Nina's RSVP so was happy for that. He had related to her about his being somewhat an outsider in the social pecking orders of things and that he and Nina spent most of their time together. He explained that the joy of that led to the hurt of breaking it off, that each part of it helped in some way to create both of them as adults.

He had told Mary about Nina when he came back to Hawaii, along with his one sea bag and an invoice for one 1960 Triumph 650 Thunderbird, to be delivered to the port within thirty days. It was as if Nina's memory came in tow with the rest of him, and she had to know of it. It made for uncomfortable conversation at first then it was done, as if he needed to purge her out of his system entirely before setting up house with Mary. Nina's memory had washed up like a huge wave, crashed into the sand with its teeming sound of sand being pummeled and washed hard, then receding back into the sea just a memory like all the other waves before and after it.

He felt that he had to tell her. That he'd be dishonest if he didn't. He had come with a minimum of baggage physically, but with steamer trunks in tow mentally. So he spat it out and then the taste was gone, and he felt that he could honestly kiss Mary now, with no trace of Nina's presence behind him. Nina had been an invisible third party to romance, and now no more. So long ago it seemed.

She listened to him breath more now. He had complained of feeling tired lately and figured maybe he needed to start walking more; the idea of swimming was too much. Maybe getting into his age for men it started. Hair loss, although he couldn't complain, weight, and yes, he had put on some extra pounds, but he wore it well.

They started getting more hair on their backs and losing testosterone, she knew. He had been healthy enough for ED medicines and when he used them hoping to surprise her, she had taken a pass at least a few times wondering what he did with his erection. He'd make these secret rendezvous and fail to alert her, she laughed sadly now. This had happened so spur of the moment and so tenderly; he hadn't a chance to take a pill. She didn't care, still feeling good.

He hadn't touched that bike in the workshop, the Triumph he wanted to fix up. Mary thought of the funeral for his brother in the 80's after the accident he had racing, and then played back a few of the funerals...weddings...christenings...baptisms. She thought of their son Drew, back on Oahu in grad school at UH for Ocean Engineering, having fallen in love with the island when a child. She smiled when Tom insisted they give him the middle name 'Kohanomoku' for Duke, the surfing champ of Hawaii, his statue erected so close to the place on the sea wall where Mary had first set eyes on Tom. He was so silly; Tom was, about things like that. Not his father's name, not his brother's name, and no one from her side, who mostly all had some pidgin nickname or something. It had to be a point of reference in their history. Something he could always think and feel inside.

They were together tonight and for her that mattered a great deal. It brought many good memories back like the hassle of starting his bike when it finally showed up at the area where they delivered vehicles at the port; uncrating it, adding gas and oil, reconnecting the battery, adjusting valves here and there. It was not unlike their marriage in some ways…constant adjustments, adding this, adding that, false starts, and flooding the engine. But the pure pleasure on his face when it kicked over and she heard the twin pipes, a private and fine memory for Mary to have. She had never seen such a wide and genuine smile on a man's face before.

Then she knew, she had more competition from that bike than any memory of some skinny blonde haole girl. He had told her about that girl, and it had taken a long time. Over the years her shadow would reappear in some book she found in a box with a dedication from the 60's, or early 70's, or in a conversation of some movie they saw taken from a novel she had given him, or a discarded box from his dad's house after he passed, filled with immature poems idolizing her. Jesus H. Christ, she wondered why he even went to school with all the damn books she shoved in that man.

She rubbed his head as he slept. What am I competing with now, haole boy?

Chapter Twelve

Nina awoke to an empty house. The stillness when she opened her eyes was something she always hated. She wished Art had left the television or the radio on, or at least the iPod in the docking station playing something. It reminded her too much of rehab. The quiet, padded surfaces allowing nothing to bother her when she became conscious. Remembering where she was; a soft landing zone for those who fall the farthest and fastest. It was pristine silence that many would kill for, but for Nina, it would have made the stay that much better to wake to *Street Fighting Man*.

She had filed against Cameron before she went in to the plush, gated house in the Santa Monica Mountains, but he was fighting the papers. Plus, he was still drinking and using so her parents had sworn out a RO against him. He was arrested at the gates of the facility one night, trying, with their connection, Phil, to scale the fence and rescue her. When she got the story, she laughed hard, picturing him being taken away. Tom would have sprung her easily, the bike hidden off the road somewhere, she mused. She used his memory as a buttress against Cameron's jealousy and rages. In her memories, Tom was still nineteen or twenty. She hadn't seen him in years, so seeing him as a man now was beyond her. The last time she saw him before rehab was when she started working at the studio and he'd gone into servitude as a seaman.

"Never shoulda let you read Conrad or Maugham," she laughed bitterly, when he told her.

"Just hope you're okay and things are good for you."

She saw where this was going. She looked and sounded like a bitch, and he was being magnanimous and humble. "And you too, Tommy." She had only called him 'Tommy' when they made love or kissed, and saying his name that way had an immediate effect on him, she knew.

Was it some sort of signal to him, he wondered? Why'd she do that? Did he make a mistake?

She continued, "You probably did the right thing. I don't think either of us are college material, not after all our weirdness…" she laughed. It was a forced laugh of soft music and shaded lights. Inside, she was angry and wanted to hit him. What a waste for him to do this.

"I want to write you…is it okay?" He asked.

She wasn't as yet engaged, but she and Cameron were practically living together, so she thought it a bad idea. "Maybe. If you send it to my folk's house only, okay?"

He nodded. He understood the clandestine nature of that request and decided he would use all his power not to communicate. And he didn't. She had to get his address from his dad, who wouldn't give it out until his brother called her back and gave her the address. And she only wrote him to tell him she was getting married.

She wanted to hurt him. He hurt her by disappearing like that. In some selfish way, in her feeling of love for him, still needing him to stay and be around. She had been without him for a long time and hadn't needed him at all, yet with his declaration of leaving, permanently, setting up house in the Bay Area and being a merchant seaman, she was angrier than a nest of wasps. Not that she could or would invite him to the wedding, that was out of the question, but she wished he were *there* somehow, even if ethereal.

He wrote her one letter before he left for Oakland, where he had found a studio off of Lake Merritt. In it he wrote:

"Abra forgave her father."

It shamed Nina to read that. She had always fancied herself a part of Abra, after reading her first, then seeing her in the movie, an awkward yet strong child-woman. Abra had thrown away the $3000 ring her father had saved years for, yet she 'forgave' him…Tom had asked very little, and yet she felt a huge hole inside her. SHE COULD LEAVE HIM. But he couldn't leave her, and he was going now. He had been there after leaving Averill that night. Now, there was no fallback, no soft spot. Why was she thinking this shit, so many years later?

She pulled herself out of bed and prayed the coffee had been left on. She didn't mind it bitter or overheated; it had character by then. Walking into the kitchen in her jammies she smiled at Art, knowing her as she saw a half pot that while the light was out, needed only a good reheat to get up to snuff.

After fixing her coffee and toasting a bagel, she sat down at the computer and started looking at the news, then logged on to her e-mail and started going down the line of deletes for junk mail that had escaped the server and filter. There was another notification about the reunion and how they were extending 'early bird' fees, which meant not too many takers on that deal. Like Art had said, she and Corinne had suffered thru the 30th, and she had described it like a scene out of 'Carnival of Souls' and added their own *MST 3000*-talk track to it. Corinne had hoped to actually hook up as a couple of the guys were not too bad looking, and as times had changed, the black guys were in better shape than their lighter and paunchier brothers. Corinne made no bones about which she went with, as long as she went. She had been single for fourteen years.

She clicked on the link to the reunion and again found herself looking at his name: Tom Kelleher. Would he be alone? Or would his wife accompany him? Art had stated right away, no way in hell would he be a part of it and have to have her introduce him to a bunch of people he didn't know and could give a flying fuck about. He didn't want to hang on her 'gun arm' if need be.

His name, just seeing it…. aroused her. Nina started to feel hotter at his memory. She hadn't thought of Tom in a long, long time … but he was never far away, sometimes so close she could make out his outline in the mist of her memory, and other times … closer. After she found him on Face Book and saw what he looked like as a man, she wasn't shocked at all. With some people you expected them to turn into eggs or old mules, but she never expected that of him.

Her own Face Book page had a picture of her with her arm

around her son at his graduation so that she didn't have to post a picture of herself alone, solitary for people to really look hard at, to study. But Tom had posted a picture of himself taken at, what was probably, his workshop, with a bike up on a special jack for work, the tank removed, engine exposed. She couldn't tell…Norton, Triumph? He was smiling, and his hair was longer and seemed to be intact, looking like he ran a hand thru it before the picture was taken. He looked happy. His face a little fuller, yet even with white hair looked virile.

She had studied pictures of Mary, the dark and island looking Mary and his son before, but not this morning. She could shut her eyes and think of him between her legs and always it would excite her. Remembering *Razor's Edge* when Isabel looked at Larry Darrell's arm in the car, focused on it as if it were the only part of a man she would ever desire, and as Maugham watched her stare, she had an orgasm. Nina let it happen now, in the still of her house, the only sound was her breathing, and then letting go in a short hard burst of sex. She laughed and said, "Fuck you, Tom," not without affection, before she took a shower.

Nina had met Art one night when she had gone out with Corinne. He saw her before she saw him. He'd been divorced for a long time and had a decent relationship with his kids and ex-wife. He'd been in the process of rediscovering himself during this time. He lost weight and looked healthier, and although the Porsche still had some bondo patches, he was restoring it nicely, like the song said, little by little.

Living up in Laurel Canyon, he wouldn't stray too far, sliding down the hill and taking in some music at a club, or eating along the Strip. That night he went to the Raincheck Room, as they had a great jukebox and the bartenders knew him and took care of him. Nina had been convinced by Corinne to have a night out. After things blew up with Cameron, she'd left the house in the hills, the "bar window" place as Chandler had darkly referred to them. She returned home before again finding work and getting her own place in West L.A. She'd seen a few men on and off, but with no success in finding anyone who could balance intellect with common sense. Lotharios she did not need. Corinne had stuck with her since her Revere High and UCLA days, a trusty sidekick. So Corinne picked her up, and they went to a few places, and then ended up at the Raincheck for pretty much the same reason Art had gone there. The jukebox.

"It's the only decent place to hear some Stones," she told Corinne. She hadn't had an alcoholic drink in some time and had just ordered a ginger ale when she saw Art looking at her.

Corinne saw him too. "That bald guy has some Yul Brynner thing going on big time."

"Don't know if I want to be a part of the *Magnificent Seven* tonight," Nina laughed, but liked his look all the same.

Corinne deadpanned as she took her mouth off her straw, "Yul, incoming."

Art had gotten off his stool and worked his way to them in the bar area. He had no clue of what to say or do, but knew he was drawn to her. Something inside him had flipped that switch of attraction, and her look caught him deep, like the perfectly placed hook on a game fish, no escape. It was time to make a fool of himself again.

"Hello, I'm Art," he said, smiling, confident and ready to tilt at windmills.

"Nina, and this is Corinne." They were both loud as the music was keyed up and the crowd was somewhat thick. "Hi Corinne," he said not caring if she dropped dead at his feet.

"Oh sorry, I thought you were Anita Pallenberg," he said and walked back to his seat.

The two women looked at each other, shaking their heads in confusion. *What just happened?* Nina took her ginger ale, and walked over to him, pawing her way through the crowd.

"Hey, I thought you were Yul Brynner, but I wasn't upset when you weren't. Well, maybe a little."

Art smiled, "I got you away from Corinne, didn't I?"

"Do you know Anita Pallenberg?"

"Not in the least, but you certainly look better than she does," he said, nodding at Corinne who stood alone, over to the side of the entry. "Your friend is starting to look like a hat rack. Better bring her over."

She liked his sense of humor right away, that droll kind of sarcasm she enjoyed. When he asked for a date, she was receptive. She didn't sleep with him that night, or the second date. She wanted to see if he had patience and rigor. Self-control. On the first date they went to see a movie in Westwood, one of her haunts with Tom, and then to a small dinner at an intimate Italian place on Pico. They swapped stories of discarded spouses and bad bosses.

He studied her as she slid around the aperitif order and asked for a sparkling cider instead, and he never brought it up, feeling that was a sore area to expound upon. He ordered wine with dinner and had an after dinner cognac. He did not want to change what he was either to suit her profile. She lived near the twenty-four hour market on Robertson so on the way home they stopped and got a donut, her confessing that she had an elaborate sweet tooth. Then he drove her back to her place and wondered if the door were open yet, not pushing it. She leaned over the stick of the Porsche and kissed him.

"I'm glad you got a chocolate donut, I can't taste the cognac. I can't taste alcohol anymore, Art." She confessed.

"No problem." And he meant it.

"I'm damaged goods. I wanted to tell you up front. I've had some issues."

"Haven't we all?"

"Seriously, I've been in rehab. I won't lie to you. If you want to get serious, that's the deal. I will be straight. If you're just looking to bounce on and bounce off, I'm not there."

"I had somewhat planned on that...but yea, I can deal with serious, too."

"Okay, then let's make another date."

They did and he kept his word. He took it seriously.

Chapter Thirteen

After she and Tom had physically and emotionally parted, Nina had been seeing Averill for months and had even started working part-time with pay at the gallery. He had an apartment across from the Palisades on Ocean Avenue and San Vicente, and her life had changed in many ways since parting with Tom. She felt as if she were coming into real womanhood. Her tastes, knowledge, appetites were things she viewed with curiosity now, wondering how far she could push her personal envelope. With Tom, she felt childlike and growing. With Averill and his friends and contacts, she felt grown and fearless.

She asked herself why it had seemed so easy to cut the rope with Tom and become someone in this lifestyle. She knew if she were capable of that, she could do what she felt. It had nothing to do with her feelings for Tom, as she felt about him after leaving as one might feel about a beloved possession they'd grown out of or away from and it had its respective place in their history, yet wasn't useful anymore. The memory was comforting and the need for that memory was thought of less and less. She also felt like she had to do this and in one way that he couldn't be a witness to or apart of this aspect of her life. At times, she pictured him as a phantom on the sidelines, laughing at her, falling back on the Holden Caulfield 'phony' that he and she had laughed at after she had him read *Catcher in the Rye* and they talked about the phonies and poseurs they saw when out. He wouldn't get it or understand what she needed now. Sex was different too. Averill introduced her to many new things…toys and drugs. She would have probably died of embarrassment if Tom had offered her a toy and asked to watch, but she found herself letting go in different ways with Averill and enjoyed being the center of attention. She knew she wasn't in love with him and that, she felt, allowed her to separate from her inhibited side. What had seemed intensely spontaneous with Tom, now looked like two kids sneaking a cigarette behind the shed, scared of being caught. She also discovered that she had something different inside as well. She felt the owner of a new inner strength and a steely skin that she hadn't possessed before.

In thinking of Tom now she felt, along with her remembered affections, an almost insane cruelty. She held him responsible for holding her back and wished she had listened to her mother long ago. Averill also had drugs and that was a whole other world. Many of the people he ran with all used something. Cocaine was always available and at any opening or party they attended. It was always just given to her, and she liked that attention. There were many men who whispered in her ear when Averill was not around, and she'd smile her downturned smile and tell them what bad boys they were. There were other women at places they went, but Nina was a different entity. Her looks were an enabler she had never fully realized before, but had a feeling about when younger, as if they were a premonition she couldn't fully understand, but now did. Even her wardrobe reflected a new and more distinct persona, more feminine and adult. Her parents quietly approved.

At times, she'd think of Tom as they drove past a place they had been or a street they had ridden down on the bike. As if his transparent apparition stood sentry over these places. Once, when driving to Malibu, she remembered the night of the Dean double feature and their late ride out to the coast. How the coast smelled that night, like they were riding through a forest of kelp as she held him tight, their talk at the almost deserted coffee shop about going to Cholame through the Polonio Pass; another dream that didn't come true. As they drove by the coffee shop, she saw the row of motorcycles, men and women in leathers hanging out. She hadn't worn her leather jacket since the last time she clung to Tom on the back of his motorcycle. He was everywhere and nowhere for her. She tried to explain it to Averill, who dismissed Tom's memory as a 'kiddy thing'.

"Forget about him," he'd say.

But lately, as if she were calling him from her subconscious, he was seeping back, entering her like a fine smoke, her pores ready to receive him again. She couldn't figure out why, but then came to the conclusion that she wished she were doing these things with Tom and not Averill. Things were changing in their relationship. A few too many of his friends were coming onto her, and many were brazen about it, not being discreet when she enjoyed the entreaties of the past. There was nothing natural about the sex anymore. What had been new and exciting before; the use of coke and other things before sex now made her question why and was bored. She used the drugs so easily, never questioning, ingesting anything; that side of her was something she hadn't conquered yet.

Averill had also been different. Where he had seemed sensuous before he only behaved in a lewd manner now and objectified her openly. And there had been traces of other women, or just other *people* in his flat. A Kleenex with lipstick not flushed down, but carelessly tossed into the waste bin of the master bath. A tampon holder left in drawer. A new tube of K-Y, as there was a used, empty one on the sink top. Averill was getting sloppy, and the thought of perhaps following a man into Averill's bed disturbed her. Then there were the thoughts of Tom she had. Why was she letting him back in?

The final night she was listening to Steely Dan's *Countdown to Ecstasy*, as she watched Averill mixing her a drink. She liked that he understood how to prepare a cocktail, but she was becoming impatient with him now. It was a night they had planned to attend a huge party in Hollywood at a director's house who frequented the gallery. She was dressed, but he still had his kimono on. Nina had taken time to do her hair and had her shag cut layered perfectly. Her high-waisted, thirteen-button bells were tight and snug around her hips and thighs. She had borrowed a peasant blouse from her mother and her red fox jacket. Her hair, still thick even after the shag cut, looked beautiful lying on the reddish brown shoulders of the fox. She had taken a long time to ready herself, yet he seemed in no hurry and handed her a drink. She listened to the lyrics of the song playing and got angrier by the minute.

"When are we leaving?" She asked dully, sipping her drink. *Razor Boy* played, as though singing to her, singing of the past. Was the Razor Boy there, ready to take all of her fancy things away?

Averill turned and she saw he was nude and semi erect under his kimono robe. "I thought we could hang out a bit before going."

Nina knew then that Averill had taken a Quaalude before she got there. They usually saved them for sex, but it was obvious he was in that zone and she wasn't. She was moving away from sex with him as of late, as he kept insisting on anal sex, which she wasn't too thrilled about. He wasn't as slow and tender as Tom had been when they were teens, and Nina hadn't gone on the pill yet. Or he'd just want oral. He was also becoming somewhat violent. She wasn't in the mood for sex and really wanted to go to this party and meet people. She didn't want to walk into a room of people she didn't know having just been fucked. The last party they went to she met Dennis Hopper who talked at length about his paintings.

"Do you want a 'lude, Nina?" Averill was ever so faintly starting to get that sedated slur in his voice. The kimono was parted wide open, exposing him to her.

Only women in cages...

"No. Will you get dressed so we can go? Its way up Londonderry off the Strip, isn't it?"

"You need to mellow out, little girl...s'no big deal if we're late. Ain't no hanging matter. Take off your jacket."

He had also started using 'little girl' a lot too, and that pissed her off. Maybe he should start looking for little boys with all the anal and oral demands. And she told him so. It just blurted out harshly and with mettle in her she hadn't thought herself capable of. Averill stood crookedly, his penis now flaccid as she ripped into him. She ordered him to stow his dick, dress, and make it snappy or he could kiss her ass goodbye. She felt like the female spider, the master of that species that could at any whim devour her mate if she pleased to, or let him scamper away knowing full well what hell lay behind him. He came out of his shock.

"Don't be a little bitch...," he started.

Nina got up right next to him, "Oh no...I'm a big bitch, not a little one. Don't ever discount that status, old man. You can pull that shit on your little boys or whoever the fuck you're doing here, but shut the fuck up where it concerns me. Now dress or I can just fuck off."

Abruptly, he started to cry and apologize. Her immediate reaction was one of repulsion. She poured her drink onto the rug, went through his room, and picked out toiletry items she had left for stay over nights and wrapped them in a shirt of his she always liked and started for the door.

"Don't leave me, Nina," he sobbed "I'm sorry. I'm just a bit high. I'll dress and we can go to West Hollywood."

She left in disgust at his tears. Where was the suave European schooled art dealer? She needed a man, not some 'luded out Warhol character.

Spontaneously, she called Tom who was getting his gear together and had sat down to pull up his engineer boots before leaving on his bike from his dad's house. He had made a date with a woman he met in a bookstore and had been seeing to meet in Westwood at the Bratskellar to have a drink.

He was surprised to hear from her, as it had been months. He wasn't too sure of what to say after their last meeting.

"So, what's new?" He felt like a total idiot asking.

"Are you busy?" She was still full of adrenaline from leaving Averill's apartment and starting to shake.

Tom looked at his brother and his brother's girlfriend, Marty, watching TV. "I'm watching TV with PJ and Marty, why?" He tried to sound nonchalant and not anxiously crazy about hearing her voice. PJ made a 'P' with his fingers towards Tom for *pussy*. Tom frowned, turning his back to him.

"Wanna meet?"

He didn't bother calling what's-her-name and rode out to Gladstone's near Chautauqua, off PCH.

Nina drove over there after leaving Averill's and called him from the restaurant. She had relaxed after a drink, waiting for Tom to arrive. She had called him out of reflex. He had agreed to meet her out of reflex.

When Tom arrived, he was almost frozen solid having only a tee shirt on under his leather jacket, and the temperature was somewhere in the 50's. Never wearing a helmet, his hair, much longer now was swept back, and when he peeked in his one mirror he thought he looked like Wolfman Jack, and started pulling his hair apart to give it a non-sprayed look. He wondered if she could see him preening like this. She had never seen him with hair this long. It framed his lean face and with the added tiger claw earring he looked like a total rocker. He hadn't shag cut his hair like most men his age, so it was long, straight and thick. He wondered what she'd think.

Nina had gotten a table so she wouldn't have to sit at the bar alone, and didn't have an angle on the door, so she didn't see Tom walk in. He headed straight for the men's room dying to piss after a cold ride and walked right by her. She only recognized him by the fact he still hung his bike gloves out of his back pocket...the same light brown leather gloves she remembered, then seeing his bike patches on the coat. But this guy also had hair about three inches past his shoulders.

"Tom?"

He stopped dead in his tracks and turned. He thought he was looking at some woman in her late 20's, early 30's. It took him, what felt like a month of Sundays, to answer her. Whatever cool he could muster before walking in drained faster than taking your finger off the top of the filled straw.

Nina saw he was in cement and sat up halfway, leaned over her table, and held out a hand to drag him down. "Sit down...Jesus...where did you get all that hair? You look so different!"

He ran his hand through his hair and then sat. He was Jett Rink, she was Leslie Benedict and he was way out of his league and knew it. He felt like a kid. Her hair cut, in a red fox jacket, a turquoise squash blossom necklace made of old buffalo nickels and a thumb sized piece of blue stone, face made up…. he just looked at her and said very slowly:

"Have to piss…cold ride, back in a minute."

She nodded knowing all about that and he left. In the men's room he started shivering as he pissed, letting the cold out as well as his emotions. He had been so knee jerk in meeting her. He went to the sink and ran some water thru his hair and tried to give it some definition other than its black wedge of biker hair.

Nina ordered a sea food salad as she was starving, not eaten, hoping to grab something when she and Averill went to the house off the Strip, and hadn't thought of what Tom would want at all. So she just waited for him and thought of how he looked. So wild and different in just under a year. But seeing him from behind, the same lean legs inside faded Levi's…tonight his black jeans, with his old black jacket with the washed out Union Jack patch with the faded black and white Triumph logo above it made her tremble. Even as different as she was, it was reflexive and immediate; animal in nature.

Tom, staring at the mirror one last time, felt inside he was like a bike that had hit gravel and started sliding, taking its owner down, pinning him. He walked back out.

She looked at him and smiled when he sat down, her mouth in that Bardot crazy, happy pout he had looked at for years. *Just one night*, he said inside, *one night and then don't ever answer the fucking phone ever again.'*

"Thank you for coming, Tommy. I'm sorry it was a spur of the moment thing, but I thought of you and well…I wanted to see you."

She decided that bringing Averill into the conversation wouldn't do any good since she had seen Tom when his fuse was lit, and didn't want to go there.

He smiled and started playing with the serviette," I'm glad you did. I was just hanging out."

"I'm having a salad, are you hungry? I didn't want to order for you…even a drink."

The waiter came up with her salad and asked if the gentleman would like a menu, and would she enjoy more chenin blanc. Tom said no to food, and yes to a Guinness.

They stared at each other. A tear ran down Tom's cheek that he couldn't suck it up.

Nina reached a hand across the table and captured it, at almost his jaw line.

He had never heard her voice so tender and soothing, "I know Tommy…I know."

"I love you, Nina."

"I love you too, Tommy."

Later, he followed her with the bike up the coast, feeling the cold and at the same time taking it as if his entire life depended on his ability to withstand it. Near Trancas, there was a place that had a neon *vacancy* sign that she pulled into. She went in and paid for the room as he shut down the bike and switched off the gas.

Chapter Fourteen

"For fucksake, Tom! The millimeter sockets, not fucking inches! Get your head outta yer asshole," PJ said. "Jesus! Get over it, will you?"

Tom handed him the whole case, exhaling from his cigarette. "Shove it up your ass." Tom had been working at the Port of Los Angeles and Long Beach in the shipyards as a journeyman structural welder, and then had fallen in with merchant seamen at the bar where the shipyard guys hung out. Many were into bikes and a few were patched up as well. They kidded him about riding a 'Limey' bike and why in hell didn't he ride a Harley? He was pulling down good money and had cratered at SMCC, going nowhere. His days were full and busy and the nights were times he'd just relax and read when he wasn't being a serial fornicator. He had filled the era that he now deemed as the *Dead Time* with women.

PJ had moved out and was splitting time between home and his new place with his girlfriend, Marty. He found a place in the Valley, but the house was a shithole needing serious work. What it did have was a garage, so he could work on his car and bikes for side money. It was an ass-haul to get there, yet Tom would go to lend him a hand and drink free beer. They were trying to fix the rear tire on a Norton café racer when Tom decided his help was over with and told PJ so much, throwing his rag into the bin and walking out.

◎◎◎

"Thanks, fucker," He spat at his back, Tom not looking around. Marty saw him as he walked up the driveway to where he parked his Thunderbird. "Leaving, Tommy?"

"Left."

Tom goggled up and kicked it over and sped off, the cigarette in his mouth disintegrating as he sped towards Sepulveda, the heat of Reseda like a brick oven. He wanted to reach the top of the pass and ride the long downhill into west Los Angeles and feel the thermo cline of the ocean air.

The Dead Time.

He was seeing three girls on and off. The half German-Chinese girl, Lise, who danced ballet, the divorcee in Seal Beach, who when he drank too much asked her to cover him in roses, but being twenty years older didn't understand the allusion, and the woman from the bookstore. Of the three, he sexually enjoyed the ballerina the most as she was fit and amazed him with how she did the splits nude. He had asked her to do it, and bashfully at first she had acquiesced, and he wondered why he had never asked Nina to do that. But she lived with her strict Chinese mother and it was touch and go making contact. The divorcee, Celeste, happened when he had stopped at a bar in Seal Beach looking for a guy, who was going to tell him about the apprenticeship program in getting a ship; but the guy wasn't there, and they struck up a conversation. Tom had never been to bed with a woman so much older than him and it was sort of out there, but he went for it since she was open to it, too.

As of late though, she'd become too attached to him, and he had tried to untangle himself from that; like a sailor fouled in line, he actually feared an injury if he didn't do the *Harry Holt, and take a bolt* as one of the Australian guys called it. He had never felt like that before, where being able to just dismiss people had been so simple. He just didn't give a shit anymore, and when she got teary, he cursed the second he laid eyes on her. But on some nights when he was torqued on a few Guinness', he'd drank with his dad or with guys at work, he'd gun it into her driveway, her waiting like his mom after school, ready to give him a snack. Then disgusted, he'd saddle up and ride into the dead of night, questioning his sanity and how weak he was, cringing inside, and needing her when he was so full of booze.

The bookstore woman intrigued him the most. She was thirty and what he termed, very calmly pretty. There was nothing ostentatious about her at all, just a natural beauty and what he felt was *earthy*. He had come into the store looking for some stuff that was a continuation of books Nina had told him he should read. He was having problems finding John W. Campbell's works and really wanted to read the short story "Who Goes There?", that the movie *The Thing* was taken from. Campbell was some serious guy she told him of in the 1930's when science fiction was really catching steam.

Lauren knew about Campbell right away and since they had a huge selection of used paperbacks, helped him locate some works by

Campbell and the story Tom sought in an anthology of his stories. Tom was very impressed with her knowledge of literature and had listened to her wax about other sci-fi writers he hadn't heard of. They also had a bevy of old, out of circulation Jim Thompson books he had also started getting into, Nina giving him a beat up copy of *The Grifters* with a 1950's print date.

"Man, where do you guys get this stuff?" he asked amazed.

She said quietly "Many people just die and their families find these books and bring them in." *Dead Men's books in the Dead Time*, he mused inside. He asked her out that very day and she agreed to meet for coffee only. They met at a place near her small apartment on Fountain and Vermont, and after talking about books took a walk. She asked him about motorcycles and he tried his hardest to leave it deck plate and not get wrapped around the axle of motors and such, but his enthusiasm impressed her.

Nina had loved his bike with all her heart, but if he had attempted to explain anything about its machinations, she'd turn the conversation to more knowledgeable climes. Lauren listened intently, enjoying his use of hands to describe cornering and downshifting, and why the two shouldn't happen at the same time. She was attracted to his face and thick straight hair, almost indigo it was so black. She admired his lean, yet strong body, and how he walked, sort of in gunslinger smoothness, like that bald cowboy in the movies. She had lived with a man for three years when in school and they were engaged, but when school ended, so did they. Having a degree in literature, started teaching for a bit and then decided she didn't want to teach after all. Her outlook shifted when she discovered that almost the entire time they had lived together, he was seeing other women, even getting too familiar with a precocious twelve-year-old next door, and then heard through an alumni sister that he had been arrested for molesting a child. She avoided her five-year reunion and fell into a funk. She had a sizable amount of money left in a trust fund and took the job in the bookstore as a place to just 'be'.

The bookstore was convenient and she could talk about books all day and anyway, she thought now, checking out Tom, I met him. She had no delusions about Tom, staring at him, while admiring him as a man, as someone who would just be passing through her life…here and gone; absolutely no expectations. And she had no illusions that she was exclusive either, not allowing herself to be in that position again. He told her exactly what he did and where he worked, not wanting to bullshit her, but didn't mention he was seeing other women. They had nice, quiet nights at her place drinking wines and listening to Eric Satie, Bert Jansch, and Mose Allison. Tom listened to many of her jazz albums as well, since he had never really got into anything but the Stones, Bob Dylan, and Robert Johnson, and of course, the man, Link Wray; music to work on motorcycles by.

Lovemaking with Lauren felt good and natural to him, but it was starting to wear him down. She'd slip into a nighty or a sleeping gown after they were done and start to rig her house for sleep time. Tom felt like they should go out again, or stay up and listen to more music. He allowed it to happen in the beginning, but started to chafe when he felt the need to stay up and talk more. So he started putting off sex, using that to ensure they'd just communicate. At times, he missed the memory of Nina, when her folks were away, and demolishing the kitchen after lovemaking as she concocted something for them, or dragged out a cookbook, and the two of them made middle of the night runs to the market to get whipping creams or skirt steaks or ingredients for a stew. It was as if the sex ignited them inside and their need for living increased. Walking up the aisles in the twenty-four hour store, his hand down the ass of her pants or her feeling him up as they looked over cantaloupes. Or they'd jump in her car when they could and fly out to the beach and watch a sunrise, her tape deck playing *Let it Bleed*, like the album sleeve had advised, very loudly.

With Lauren, as much as he felt attuned to her soul, she started feeling soporific to him. There was no spontaneity or whimsy. Her flat resembled very much the bookstore with old wooden bookcases full of editions, some old and probably rare bound books, and many dozens of paperbacks. Sometimes, without the cover of patchouli incense she liked to burn, it smelled like *the* bookstore inside. She rode on the back of his bike once and never asked again, and he didn't offer. There was some sort of dread sometimes, living inside her, that creeped him out. She asked about the absence of sex, and he just lied and said he was a guy that it wasn't that important for.

He found himself riding from east Hollywood to the beach and the ballerina on nights he needed a connection. His divorcee was too far away down the coast, and he was trying to wean himself away from her, loathing what he felt when he gave in and showed up on her front door, her disgust almost matching his, yet letting him inside. And there were others outside the troika he was drawn by, random pickups, and run ins. Behind Picwood Bowl on the seat of his bike with the bartender who showed him her tattoos or the secretary near the shipyard in the merchant seaman's hall with huge breasts he just couldn't stop playing with.

The Dead Time, where he was alone and stared at the ceiling in the dark and in his cigarette smoke envisioned Nina, and thinking of her, wondering. He knew she was seeing other men or a specific man, and had once even spied on her at the gallery she hung out at in Santa Monica. He almost called up and put on a phony accent to hear her voice, but was again disgusted at his need, and succumbed to his inner child and went to Seal Beach instead.

The days blurred and spun by, work, sex, bikes, and work. His father was happy that he was working steady and seemed to start living without Nina, who had been a fixture since he was fourteen.

Then the phone: "Wanna meet?"

Chapter Fifteen

Nina took on some freelance work now and again, small bits of dialogue, or whole scripts, dependent on who remembered her work and who also knew her limitations. She didn't bite off huge chunks of editing work anymore, but she took enough to keep her in what Art termed 'beer money'. She had a good ride during the late 70's and into the 80's despite her return for what she ruefully termed her relapse tour. She just took little bites and ingested work without too much heartburn.

She was grateful for those who remembered her before her union with Cameron became toxic on many levels. Today she decided to take her work valise and head down to the bookstore café in Venice and do some work outside, enjoying the salt air and freak show the boardwalk promised on a daily basis. When there, she'd religiously walk down and put a dollar in the crumpled hat of the toothless old whore who sang *Love for Sale* on the Boardwalk at Navy Street. Walking away she'd almost always muttered in her head, *there but for the grace of God*....

After showering and grabbing a croissant, she drove out to the beach. She and Art had a beautiful cottage in a very secluded area of Brentwood, so she took San Vicente west which was convenient and made a left turn at Ocean, passing old ghosts and headed south to Venice. The day was sunny and although a little brisk, she put the top down so she could smoke. Her lungs needed a bite so she started smoking Lucky Strikes, and as she drove, felt wonderful with the wind taking what hair wasn't tied down into a spin around her head, white and golden in the sun as if wearing a crown of heraldry.

She was on Ocean now and was in the right-hand lane at the entrance to PCH, stopping at the traffic light. When it turned green, she pulled the wheel and started down the onramp onto the coast highway, just going with her inner thoughts and memories:

Tom Kelleher.

She pointed the car north on the on the coast highway noting many streetlights and roadside business had been added since the days they flew up and down the coast either in her VW or on his bike. Now it was a waste to come down here as a means to blow out the pipes and speed up the coast. But they'd stop for coffee on almost every corner. Gone were Thelma Todd's place, and all the weird broken structures on the mountainside of the road. She wondered if Tom had been back in LA and had driven up the coast, seeing what monumental changes had taken place. Sometimes they hung at Sorrento Beach, the north side of the pier or at T's. That had changed as well with a lot of new construction and the disappearance of the old beach club. The whole city had changed, and it was no wonder they unearthed so many ancient cities under cities in Europe. They just kept piling the shit higher and higher, she thought to herself.

How weird would it be to share this drive right now with Tom?

Did he still ride bikes? She had seen his Face Book page and the bike on the stand he looked like he was retooling, but maybe it was just a pose. She hoped he did, remembering his hair dovetailed by the wind, years before the helmet laws were in effect; that idiot actor cracking his skull on a curb and the kneejerk reaction to finally enforce a law. She never wore a helmet back then and certainly wouldn't now. No way would her hair look right!

Playing hooky, she drove up to Malibu and stopped at Duke's. She'd do a little work here after a Caesar salad and maybe some seared *ahi*, and then head back into town. She stepped out of the car and could really smell the kelp beds today, igniting her mind. She and Art had eaten at Duke's in Waikiki, and even there, Tom crept through her thoughts. Thoughts of him living there for so many years, knowing he was married there, and had a son born there as well. When Tom was in her head, it was never wraithlike, but a good solid thing she could hold to, comforted by the substance of it. His article was never malignant, nor was it some fanciful and angelic presence either. Just him, for all he was worth. Her 'shanty Irish' boyfriend as her father would amusedly describe him to her mother, bringing his Protestant feelings to bear.

She ordered her food and drinking an unsweetened tea, opened her valise to get out the property she was working, but then deciding instead to write him, she sent him a message in Face Book. It just said hello. And then, she thought, *Let the devil take the hindmost.*

She had let the devil do that many times before, so why stop now?

Chapter Sixteen

Tom sat in his office at school, doodling on a legal tab just drawing faces. Some were fat, others thin. One had a pig nose, another a beak. He wasn't drawing anyone in particular, just how he felt about everyone in general. He didn't care. He looked at the wall across from his desk, next to the door where his Saint-Exupery quote hung:

"What is essential is invisible to the eye"

What is it I can't see? Was it something to do with Mary? Was it the problem he was suffering from his shipyard days, working in areas of severe dust and asbestos where they tore down the lagging wrapped around the piping systems? Was it someone's birthday? He shut his eyes, hoping to see the thing in there he couldn't see with his eyes open. He saw Steve McQueen sitting on his Triumph in *The Great Escape* that hung to the left of Saint-Exupery. Then he concentrated and started thinking of things that weren't in his office. Mary's lingerie, the yard, and the garage workshop...damn he was boring. He opened his eyes. He had a small bulletin board that had this and that stapled or pinned to it. He had one card on the bottom right of James Dean, standing with the rifle across his shoulders in the crucifixion pose from *Giant*. Under it someone had taped a small sign that said 'live fast'. One of his students from a few semesters ago had hung it there, and he left it, no reason to take it down. Dean. Immortal. Kelleher. Under sentence.

Maybe if he smoked a pipe, he'd see himself becoming pensive, stuffing it with tobacco, and readying it for a match…but he didn't smoke a pipe. Pipes opened up thought for big things. Whenever he saw a guy load up a bowl he'd elbow Mary and say, that guy is on the verge of a breakthrough or something to that effect. What was he on the verge of here?

He rolled back into thinking of immortality. In his Intro to Humanities class, they were discussing the Greeks and Troy came up. So, allowing each class to stretch its arms so to say, he green lighted some conversation and dialogue. He enjoyed when they took the reins and just ran; some fresh out of high school and feeling their oats. He was already well into his twenties when he went back to school in Hawaii and argued with his professors, many of whom had gone from school into teaching without having lived or done anything else. So he let his own students run free for a bit. The meme du jour was about immortality and how one attains it. The argument found its origins in Homer and they talked at length of the Greeks and Trojans and how their story was repeated so many times, in the *Iliad* and *The Odyssey* in so many languages and films. *Troy* had just come out and most had seen it already, so they centered on Achilles and Hector. They directed disdain for Helen and Paris, who although they were the catalyst for the Trojan War, they were what one wag in class termed 'passive immortals'. They weren't as heroic as the others. Paris certainly didn't deserve to kill Achilles. Tom interrupted here to ask what of the nameless Greeks and Trojans who perished in the ten years of war? What claim did they have to immortal pastures? None! Said the wag. They had to be identified, and they had to die importantly or foolishly.

So Tom asked the class, "How can we obtain Immortality? We're just a bunch of people that showed up for class, and then maybe go to our jobs somewhere. We do our laundry and shop for food. Just being a God, won't ensure it," he claimed. "Who remembers Demeter, the God representing Virgins? Nobody is going to build a Taj Mahal for me," he added with a smile. "When my immediate family leaves this mortal coil, who will remember me, really? I'll just be some old guy in a picture. Then my memory will fade away forever. So what can we do to ensure some form of immortality?"

"Die really cool!" Came a shout from the back of class.

You can always count on freshmen; he smiled, and started looking back.

◎◎◎

Nina and he were discussing Brian Jones and the news of him being found tits up in his pool. It was already July 1969, and they were out of school and just killing the days at the beach or listening to music at night and hanging at some parties. Jones was their favorite musician, and his image lent itself to what they sought in their heroes at that age. The news was also disturbing as it sent a warning and a reality bite of what happened when you were careless. They lay across her bed, under the fan in her above garage loft. Nina had a full poster of Jones walking through the Monterrey Pop festival on her bedroom wall. And as they both lay across her bed, they looked at it upside down. Tom had always told her she looked like Jones's old girlfriend, Anita Pallenberg.

"Well...he's gonna be immortalized like Dean and Buddy Holly. None of these guys have died a natural death," Tom stated. "No Jones, no Stones... What the heck is 'death by misadventure'...?"

"Yup. He was so beautiful...but you always sort of knew he wouldn't see thirty" she said. "I loved his guitar playing."

"So who's next?"

They spent awhile throwing out names of those who might go at any time or could certainly use a little help. "Keith Richard can't be far behind," Tom weighed in. "None of the Beatles...those guys will live a long time," Nina said. "Ginger Baker for sure...he looks on the verge of death daily."

Tom rolled over and started running his finger across her exposed stomach as he lay propped up on one elbow, looking at her finely shaped *inny*. It was tickling her and she started to giggle and push his hand away.

"You'll always be immortal for me, Nina...always."

She took his hand and placed it inside her shorts, opening her legs, "Yes?" she smiled. "Make love to me, mortal."

And he obeyed.

◎◎◎

He smiled remembering that day and then in review of those they had picked out to die, and how woefully off they were, and gave a chuckle. He leaned over and reaching out, with fingertips pulled the Dean card off the bulletin board and brought it to bear. He and Nina listened to the Eagles too, and he thought of their song *James Dean*. He remembered the lyrics out of nowhere, not having even thought of the song or heard it in years and he sang/talked it…'along came a Spyder, picked up a rider…' He realized he'd never driven a Porsche in his life.

He never got to Cholame with Nina. The closest they ever got was the motel on coast Highway just outside Trancas. That seemed like a million miles from Cholame and the Polonio Pass. And it's fifty-four years this year since he died. Wow! Feeling old here, he muttered and left his office to get some coffee at the small teachers mess they had in the lounge in his department.

He gazed out the window and saw that all of the snow had melted. That late storm had dumped and then just blew out. They got them at times in late March and early April. Spring would be all over the place soon, and in D.C. the cherry blossoms would be on display. Mary and he liked to train down into the city and see them, walk on the mall, see what was on exhibition. He also had his calendar set for April to attend his 40th reunion, and maybe look around Los Angeles for a day, check it out. He also had an appointment the next week with his doctor to start discussing a plan. They had pinpointed his work in the Navy yard when he was a scrub, and they were pulling lagging down off the overhead pipes. Whatever, he still needed to sit down and tell Mary, and he hadn't done that yet. How do you open that conversation? It was a total cliché.

When he started to feel sorry for himself he walked down the usual avenues of male egocentricities and drank at that bar for a while.

Would she remarry? Is my hair going to go away? Would she always remember me? What about my son? Maybe I won't ever see grandchildren? He got sick of it after a bit, mentally kicking himself in the ass.

He thought of PJ and his accident and how barely a year later, Marty had moved in with his best friend Ray, selling all of his tools and racing gear, not even offering anything to Tom. The memory was still cold. Tom had been estranged from PJ for a long time too, so maybe…who knows. He probably told Marty to fuck him and not leave him anything. Tom shook his head at where his mind was wandering. Idiot!

He kept circling that class session about immortality. Everybody was on YouTube now explaining their personal 'bucket lists' and what they wanted to do before they croaked. So for him to do that, he felt very lame. Anyway, what if after they gut him and make all his hair fall out, he lives?

He finished his coffee, was tired of this mental jerking off and returned to his office.

The crucifixion picture of Dean was on his desk still, and he wondered if he should toss it or place it back on the board. Deciding it wasn't a major decision; he picked it up and tossed it onto the corner of the desk. He looked at his computer screen and saw that he had a notice from Face Book, figuring Drew was sending a picture of him surfing somewhere to piss him off on the east coast. But it wasn't Drew.

Nina had sent him a simple message: "Hello."

Chapter Seventeen

When he and Nina entered the motel on the coast at Trancas, there was what they jokingly called, the pregnant pause, while they closed the door and started to put their things down. They hadn't said a word since entering and cautiously just avoided any contact. Tom slipped off his leather jacket, still freezing, and then wished he had put on a different shirt. He felt very under dressed next to her. Nina looked like a total woman. In his biker clothes and wife-beater tee shirt, he felt like the paperboy.

She was turned to the side, and he watched her in profile. He sat down on the bed, making noise, and she turned to him. Her fox was off and she had pulled her hair back away from her face. The lamp on the chest of drawers under the small portable television was of low wattage. The area around it that Nina was in threw light on her that made an enormous shadow on the wall over the double bed. Tom saw how really small the room was and how old. As he looked at her, he did what he always did before bed, emptying everything that was in his pockets. Change, lighter, bike key, gloves, wallet, and he placed them on the small table in front of the picture window of the room.

Nina took a cigarette from her leather and fringe beaded bag and tamped it on the top of the TV before placing it in her lips. She rummaged through her purse until Tom, shaken from his fixed position, grabbed his lighter and moved to her side. She held his hand as she puffed in the flame. He had got it on one of the ships he'd been working on, the *U.S.S Belleau Woods.*

"Where did you get this?"

"Work. I work in Long Beach and San Pedro now…shipyards…" the words dropping off as he spoke. She gave him a brief incredulous smile.

They were close now, and he saw the light in her eye closest the weak lamp. The grayness had small flecks of rust like staggered spokes around the pupil. It was what she had termed a holdover from her Scandinavian roots; her flaw in the iris. She first pulled down her bottom eye lid when they were virginal fourteen-year-olds and asked him to look in like it was one of those big deals when you started to share with your puppy-love crush personal items of interest.

He peered into her eye then and saw the color difference, and also how the gray was patterned with areas that were lighter or darker and not all uniformly monotone. This was the closest he had been to someone's eyeball and he was interested. They were sitting on her couch, in the living room of her parent's house, while her folks watched TV in the den, Tom pushing himself on his hands to get a higher aspect and look down into her eye. That was so many years ago…

She stared back up at him as he looked down into her eyes.

"You're looking at my iris. The darker part."

"Yes, I am." He was erect in his jeans, and she knew it without looking. She took a drag on her cigarette, then turned it, and held it for him. Her left hand moved to his thigh and she held his cock that way, her fingers outstretched on it. He shut his eyes slow at the contact, letting the smoke out easy, he put the lighter down and ran his right hand over hers, pushing it against him harder, wanting her to not just touch him, but feel his heat. His other hand started unbuttoning her blouse. She looked around for an ashtray and Tom took the cigarette and dashed it on the top of the TV, extinguishing it in a small shower of ash and sparks.

Both said nothing, knowing that words were useless now, and her hand sliding up and down him as he used both hands now pulling her blouse down over her shoulders. They looked whiter to him than they had been. She hadn't been to the beach at all, and he stopped himself from wondering why. He leaned and ran his tongue over her clavicle and up to her neck. Her hand, free of the cigarette, came up and grabbed a chunk of his hair, strands spilling in between her fingers as she pulled it lightly. He still wore his faded brown leather belt that she opened one-handed.

Everything was so familiar to her, and yet it seemed different too, like he was a man she just met. His longer hair, earring, and even his body, while intimate to her, seemed different, rangier and harder. He may have had the same clothes, but he looked older to her too, in his face. He kissed her neck and she pulled harder on his belt, and pulled then on his top jean buttons. She needed to feel him naked, exposed.

He opened her blouse and unhooked her until she felt the pull of the material disappear and relax. She was loose in her cups and it felt good. She wanted his hands on them, pulling, kneading, and pinching. His hands were larger than Averill's, and they were rough, and she wanted them to be rough. She didn't want anything tonight to be sedate. Her anger at Averill had wrapped her tightly, and she was coiled, a hard steel spring. She wanted Tom, all of him to unravel her and break her apart. She didn't want him to view this as some fantasy reunion of smoke and lights and classical music. She needed him to just fuck her, no Quaaludes to make her feel anything else other than Tom's lips, tongue, cock and hands.

Her hand gripped his flesh, happy he hadn't worn shorts under his jeans, as she wanted to explore him and remind herself about what she wanted and where she needed it. His hands had her bra up over her tits and her need must have translated to him somehow because he was pulling her nipples and pinching them, as he started biting her neck. She pulled him up by his hair and didn't wait to meet, but sought his mouth and kissed, biting his lips, making him squeeze her nipples harder, then take all of them in his hand and smother her tits with them.

Standing became unbearable, taking more balance than they were capable of.

Tom lifted her up and moved the foot or two to the bed and laid her down. Nina sat up and started moving up to the pillows, pulling the bed spread away, kicking it on the floor. She pulled her jeans down, arching her hips to slip them off and watched Tom undress standing up in front of her at the foot of the bed. He pulled his jeans away from his cock. Exposed it hung heavy and firm, his dark thick hair against his white skin, his stomach flat, and again she held his image against Averill. Nina had just pulled her knees up and he could see her panties inside her lips, obviously wet. He left his jeans on the floor, pulled his shirt over his head and crawled, pulling her legs wide and dragging his nails down the inside of her thighs as he lay between them, pulling the thin material away and closing his eyes at her scent. Nina's scent. He shivered at the effect she had on him and knew what her cunt tasted like. He wrapped his arms up under her thighs, lifting her lightly with his shoulder, running his hands up to hold her tits, his fingers on her nipples as he started kissing her.

She was going insane, wanting him to just eat her, use his tongue crazily and make her explode. She wanted him to bite and hurt her. Her hands were deep in his hair as she let go.

Before she could stop shaking, he was in her and they kissed each other's faces. She wrapped her arms under her legs and pulled them wide. She was thinking of what they looked like, how it felt, why she needed it, and how she needed it. She hated Averill in that moment and wished he could see her being fucked like this...how *he* wanted her to act, but Tom made *her*. How she wanted to be Tom's little fuck-baby right now, and even if he wanted to use her as a punching bag in that moment, she would've cried, *Yes!* It was wild tasting herself on his lips, thinking that she loved him and wanted him now like never before. Tom was pounding her and she knew he wouldn't last longer, she could tell by his sides and abdomen, how tense he was getting, and she knew he was up on his toes, getting ready. These things she knew. She started talking to him in a half spit, half moaning plead to cum inside her. As she whisper-moaned in his ear, they kissed frantically, and then he put his head down, again to listen to her…then screaming, he lifted her off the bed, putting his hands under her, letting it go deep inside, holding her to him.

It took a while for him to relinquish his grip and allow her some wiggle room. They were on each other's flanks, holding her aside, he just had to let himself shake and calm until he felt he could breathe without hurting himself. Nina loved to feel this secure and loved how he felt, flaccid, but still large and crushed under her ass and the tops of her thighs. She thought she could feel a weakening pulse in his softening cock, like a dying heart.

Tom woke as if he were decompressing from a huge depth of water. He slowly swirled through the thick water to the light at the surface and found that neither of them had moved at all in the time they slept after passing out, of which he had no memory. It was as if after they had exploded, he was swallowed by a darkness that he didn't see or feel coming. He was that exhausted emotionally. Waking in a strange bed was nothing new, but next to her it was exceptional. She breathed very slowly, barely audible. They were well off the highway in the room they were given, but it wasn't late enough to enjoy silence. He heard the weekend traffic streaming by, white noise. They were still on top of the sheet and blanket, the warmth from their bodies enough. Tom was fully awake now, but still feeling like he was in slow motion as he extricated himself from her and got up to piss.

In the mirror, he looked a wreck, and he badly needed a cigarette. He sat down to piss, and didn't care either. He was still rubber legged. He hadn't fucked like that since the last time he and Nina had long ago, before she left him. His trysts with the ballerina were weak in comparison…and guiltily he thought of Celeste and her Honky Tonk ass, and felt a momentary wave of nausea. He had broken off his date with Lauren this very night, even when she was taking a risk and driving far off to Westwood and his part of town to actually have a drink, and he didn't even so much as call and take a rain check. He didn't feel anything when he wondered what she had done, showing up and sitting there…maybe calling his house and PJ either covering or throwing him under the train. Either way he didn't care. He considered why he felt nothing and didn't have one idea or thought to elucidate. In one instant, he felt it was just payback for his acceptance of her lifestyle and his past acquiescence. He didn't love her and that lack of interest was mutual. She had no illusions of her association with him. Fuck it.

But now he was faced with what had just happened. He had no doubt when she woke up, she'd be thinking the same exact thing. *What next? What the fuck happened?* He had to control himself, steel his will in some instances, and not slide back into that comfortable zone he was in when he became complacent, and she started becoming his sister or partner in crime. He wondered if she would, after the smoke cleared for her, decide this was a bad idea after all and walk again. What could he say or do to dissuade her…and, did he want to dissuade her if so? *Jesus*, he mumbled, rubbing his head, wishing to eliminate the pressure he felt. He got up from the toilet and walked back into the room, really seeing how small and compact it was. Nina was on the bed, rolled over towards him, rubbing her eyes, smiling.

"You were my blanket and it woke me up when you took yourself off me." Her voice was deeper, still somewhere inside her sleep. "Where are the cigarettes?"

Tom, nude, lit two and grabbing the ashtray laid it down between them as he positioned himself on his side, up on one elbow. "I like when you do that," she said, "lighting both cigarettes. I think of Dietrich and Cooper in *Morocco*."

Tom smiled and gave Cooper's signature little twirl salute from his forehead. "There's a small convenience or liquor store down the block, isn't there? I seem to remember it." He was starving and also wanted something cold to drink.

"God yes…and if they have a bunch of junk, get some of that too…I want something sweet." Nina loved candy or Hostess Snowballs.

He dressed and went off to the store. Nina covered herself with the sheet, and smoked, glancing at the phone. Then threw off the sheet and walked into the bathroom, to be met by her visage in the mirror.

"Yikes! What happened?" she laughed, pushing her hair back. She felt fine, though, regardless of her look.

Like Tom, she looked into her own eyes and asked what and where is this going? *Was this real or just reaction?* Inside she had such strong feelings on both sides of the fence concerning Tom.

Scared of him needing her too much and scared of her falling back into the security of his constancy. She didn't look forward to the conversation after he returned with goodies from the run he was on and wanted to avoid the inevitable questions and reproach in his voice. How could she make him see that while she was sleeping with Averill, it didn't subtract from him…when she held them up against each other. Jesus, Tom could turn her hair white. His hair was wild. He seemed wilder now. He seemed together, but sort of dangerous looking and what the hell was this shipyard scene about? She shook her head. Okay, she was making things up now. She needed a drink, and she was also aroused again.

When he came back, she pulled his shivering body back into bed with her, preventing any discussion. For now.

Chapter Eighteen

She had three surfboards and let him use her long board to start out on. He had surfed in southern California, but not Hawaii. The first six months had been a honeymoon, but now, with her graduation coming up and certification and job-hunting, she was stressed and Tom was having fun. She was spending less time playing now and started to allot more hours to things she *had* to do, not necessarily *wanted* to do. The nights were pulling her apart too; she couldn't stay up as late as he wished, and he was always finding something new that he wanted to share with her. He was like a little boy, his excitement and curiosity about all things local was contagious. She hadn't been to the *heiau* in Aiea Heights in years, but let him drag her there on his bike, also walking the Loop Trail on the spur of the moment. He was full of life and desire to know so many things. She worked on one thing during this time, besides her own matriculation, getting him to enroll and having a future with him.

It was as if she were babysitting a grown man, and while they made love and discovered each other, Mary had a pragmatic endowment and had to make sure if they were going to play at playing house. It was going somewhere. She was almost done with school and there was going to be a big celebration and party at her parents in Kahuku, but she had minimally opened the door to her family about Tom and the fact he was a haole. Little steps she always reminded herself. Little steps.

She grew up, in what used to be termed before the island became so crowded, as "up country". Kahuku was way out windward on the road to North Shore, way north of Kaneohe, and the marine base. Her family was mixed with a variety of south sea islanders, local Chinese and Portuguese, who were in many ways reviled, but eh, when part of da family, no problem. Tom even started talking local pidgin from some of the surfers he hung with and people he met during the day walking along the beach or hanging out on Kalakaua.

"Man, Mary...the closest I ever got to this was watching Poncey Ponce on *Hawaiian Eye* as a kid. I even thought Robert Conrad was a Hawaiian!" He made her laugh with his simplistic island ideas from television. So haole!

So she started to fret with actually opening her life to her family. She had always dated haole guys, but she hadn't lived at home, having always had a job, since she started at UH. She knew early on that she needed to get away from the country and the microcosm of family life and those expectations. She also hated roosters and tired of hearing them crow at daybreak, chickens clucking under her window, choosing to either surf away her boredom or take the bus into town or over Haleiwa for a shave ice with her cousin Bernice. Mary was the only person, so far in her extended clan, to be accepted to UH and that was a big deal. Her Papua granny told her she was meant for big things, and Mary believed her.

She looked over at Tom as he lay in bed asleep, and at his white skin and blue-black hair, his small, upturned nose, long lashes, and firm jaw line. He was a travel poster for haoles. But, he was *her* haole, and she had made her bed. He even stopped dressing like a biker and started looking local in board shorts and tanks, his skin tanned but woefully shy of local pigmentation. She woke him and they started to talk about graduation and her getting certified as a teacher and where she might work. She also said it was time for Tom to make a decision about work or school. His playtime was done and she didn't want a guy like her Uncle Lou, who was a beach boy essentially his whole life. While playing the good times, Uncle Lou never saved enough to rescue his teeth and fathered like four kids who used the family charity. No Lou's in her life.

During her speech, Tom listened closely and also paid attention to her bracing him for the graduation and party at her home and what he might expect as serious headwinds due to his ethnicity or blank page looks.

He was okay with it and understood as she continued to warn him about him *not* speaking pidgin with her family. They'd take it as condescension and being rude, even if her cousins and extended family talked nothing but. He understood.

Her commencement was beautiful and when it was over, he found her in the circle of family members almost hidden under beautifully flowered leis of ilima, kokui and maile. Tom wasn't unprepared as he strode up and offered her pink plumeria lei; symbolic of the flower she had in her ear the night they had kissed that first time on the beach. The people around her looked at him, and her mother leaned over and asked her something he couldn't hear. Mary shook her head no, then stretching as if to clear her voice from the rows of leis said something to her mother, who in turn glared at Tom up and down, making an upside down smile of resignation. She then introduced Tom around to indifferent attitudes and finally whispered in his ear, "See you back home in a bit." So he left, nodding his head at everyone for lack of anything else he thought to do.

There were cold Coronas in the icebox and he lay on the bed listening to the neighbors through the walls, wondering what the hell he was doing. He got notice that he could return to his old job, or not. He had a brochure from a recruiter at UH he stared at absentmindedly, plus a letter from PJ about coming to help him open up a new garage in Pacoima. Pacoima? What was PJ thinking other than maybe not spending a lot on a property? Marty and he were serious. He couldn't see working with or for his brother so that was out. He'd been a sailor for over two years, and had already given up his place in Oakland. He turned his back on that life when he flew back to Oahu, shipping his bike. He loved Mary and he wanted a life with her. The family stuff would work out in time, and if they hated his guts, they'd at least love their grandchildren, so whatever it took. This week, he thought, I'll see about what I need to do to enroll and start school.

He'd never seen so much food in one place. There were picnic tables set up in the carport, with three cars, two broken, down in the yard. The street and lane running up to the small old kama'aina style house were lined with cars. Mary's car had refused to start, so she willingly agreed to ride out with Tom on the bike instead of bussing it. So they pulled up on the Triumph, Tom letting her slide off the back of the bench seat and he looked for a hard stand to put it up. After turning off the key and the gas, he dismounted and pulled off his goggles to find two local guys around him, checking out his the bike. Tom smiled and said, "Howzit?", out of reflex, forgetting what Mary had said.

"500 cc?" the one guy asked.

"650," Tom said.

"Do any racing?" The other asked, his voice sing-songing the three words.

"No, but have done some off-roading before. Bultacos and Husqvarnas. You race?"

"No…just ride off-road. Come see my one bike."

So Tom walked off with the two and Mary searched for him after kissing her parents and granny. She saw her Auntie Milly.

"Auntie, see that big haole boy I rode in with?"

"He walked away with Rommell and Kaipo, dat way," she said, pointing. Her two cousins who smoked pakalolo and pretty much wished to emulate Uncle Lou, their dad by different moms.

She found them next to Kaipo's dirt bike; a beat up Hodaka, and Tom was on one knee playing with something under the seat that had been removed.

"Eh, what get?" She asked her cousin, walking up.

"Your boyfren' *akamai*. Know his shit with one bike. He

found wiring problem *wiki.*"

Tom turned and looked up at her and then shrugged. Mary smiled back proudly and then looked at her cousins. "He *killah akamai, braddah.*"

And after surviving tons of char-su chicken, mushu pork, kalua pork rice, lau lau, spam, ribs, plate lunch style macaroni, pancet, lumpia, opakapaka, sushi rolls, portage sausage and almost trying balut from a Filipino cousin but then almost gagging, they bid everyone good night. He kicked the bike over; Mary straddled it, her teeth in his neck. They peeled away. He thought of her dad, Miles, telling him, good choice; go back to school. He explained how his real name came from a plant in New Guinea, Nikinu, but he had it changed to Miles after reading US history about Miles Standish in grade school. Mary's mom, Lokelani, backed up her husband's remark in regards to Tom's choice to go to school. When Mary had introduced him to her dark skinned granny, she smiled a somewhat toothless, but wide-open grin, and said a very broad aloha, and held his hand warmly. She pulled Mary down to her and whispered in her ear, to which Mary blushed.

Later when he asked her what she said.

She grinned and said, "Granny asked if you had a big one because in marriage that's important."

Tom laughed at her embarrassment. He asked if Mary was her real name, and she replied, yes, that her parents wanted her to have a staid, haole name, but Mele, the Hawaiian version of Mary meant "obstinacy" and "rebellion."

"That's you," he laughed.

Back home, exhausted and in bed, he got up and she thought he was going to get them a cold beer to share but instead he came back with a small, wrapped box.

"Congratulations, *wahine*."

She propped up on an elbow, "Eh, what's this? Gift for becoming a *kumu?*"

The room was fragrant with the dying flowers from the leis, and he breathed them in deeply, as he watched her, wanting to remember this occasion, and remember the smell of the flowers.

The note with the ring that was engraved with "Kuuipo", meaning sweetheart said simply, "Be my Pilialo (wife)."

"Can't afford a diamond, yet" he told her softly.

She smiled, "*Shoots* …of course." It was that simple.

Chapter Nineteen

Her work had been admired and she was enjoying some small notoriety in what she was doing. She was already out of the small independent studio and in Burbank, hating the drive but understanding what goes with the territory. Nina was confident in what and where she was going. She had received kudos for her work, back channels, and also in front of important people who liked her. Things with Cameron had taken a downturn, but she had hopes he'd extract his head from his ass soon, as she had put her foot down. Not her problem if he can't handle it.

She hadn't seen or heard from Tom in ages, and at times, would randomly wonder what and where he was. Was he married? She hadn't tried to contact him and had lost the string with his brother and didn't want to call anyway. She was married, employed, and their social circles would only in some alternative universe ever cross again, so why bother? But she did miss aspects of her relationship with him. Cameron would never be as loyal as she remembered Tom to be. Never just be there without having to insist. He wasn't hardwired that way. He was selfish and in some ways far more immature than Tom ever had been. Was it her destiny to have men who needed a strong woman, an enabler to allow them to achieve manhood?

In the cooling down period and the distance between her and Tom, she had viewed him in many different ways. He was always as she thought, a strong and consistent man, who had always been there when needed, yet he was also needy and had to have her as a 'tit' on days he needed a soothing hand and a mom. Invisible to her was the fact that she had served so much as his tutor in opening his mind and exposing him to things he had never sought on his own. To her it was just natural that she help improve the person she had so many feelings for, and was shocked years later, when Tom admitted yes, she had opened his world without realizing it and set a certain trajectory he had not ever thought imaginable. But she never viewed it that way.

Cameron was quite the opposite. He was competition and when they were sitting with friends getting high, he needed to own the conversation or breach the big ideas, pushing Nina to the edge, peripheral in any intellectual round about. Tom listened and absorbed what she said and then asked questions. She missed his collegial give and take and discussing things after they viewed them together. Cameron would at times talk to her as if she were from another country in dissecting things to make them simple, and her resentment would simmer inside until she hit a boiling point. His awareness of her intellectual abilities frightened him and he oft times wondered what came over him to try and throw a saddle on this wild horse. And at different times when he rode her during a conversation or in front of others, he'd be thrown violently and quickly to the dust, Nina kicking and jumping, smiling ruefully at him as if he should have known better and had been warned. He was still at the studio where they had met, and while making good money, wasn't enjoying the same amount of attention Nina had conjured with her prowess.

They drank a lot and then started using cocaine and heroin. She would shake her head at the cliché of working in Hollywood, using, and how two-dimensional she felt in her situation at times. She convinced herself it was part of work and helped her, and it also helped her tolerate what was becoming a disastrous union with him. They had flown to Bali for a friend's wedding and the flight was just too many hours. Cameron had used in the bathroom and she took pills to sleep. In Bali, their bags were gone through by the agents at the airport and a small amount of powder was found. It was a nightmare and they were jailed for a full day before an embassy person arrived. There were, in that time, payouts to extricate one's self from a bad situation; they missed the wedding and flew home broke, pissed-off, and at each other's throats with recriminations. It had been discussed about flying into a Hindu and Muslim country clean and enjoying themselves, yet he took along drugs. He didn't tell her and she was beside herself, yet outwardly cool and unperturbed. Back in Los Angeles, there was a cooling off period, and Cameron thought he had finally found a way out of the doghouse. Nina had been aloof, yet friendly. Sex had disappeared and wasn't part of the marriage quotient anymore, and Nina made sure it wouldn't either, extracting her pound of flesh.

She discussed her problems with her mother, who despised Cameron, as did her father who hated his name to begin with, thought it pretentious and it fit him to a tee. They recommended a separation to let things settle and also to give her a break and possibly make a getaway. Their feelings for him pushed her to naturally defend him on some level, and it also made her wish to stay sedated, and she did. When not working, she was a somnambulist in her marriage, when working a cloud of cigarette smoke, vodka, and gin tonics and in bra and panties, her work uniform. He wasn't allowed in her office at home, which at times was her bed.

At the time, they were renting a huge terraced house off Beachwood in what she called Warren Zevon territory. Listening to *Desperados Under The Eaves,* at times she felt trapped in a bad joke …"look away down, Gower Avenue…" but there was really nothing there besides her feeling morose, and she played it over and over, getting drunker and drunker.

Over time, Cameron started using more junk, and their friends started slipping away, peeling off discreetly at first, uninviting themselves from dinner or a day of swimming. Then wholesale and blatant no shows and denials of privileges; they were being treated like some toxic modern version of the Divers when Dick fell out of favor. Nina wasn't used to doors being shut and retaliated in kind. And also drank more to smooth out her own feathers. She started using Tom as a weapon, Cameron knowing full well who he was, and hated being held against the memory of some twerpy puppy love she idolized from her teenage years. She enjoyed the broadside hits that Cameron took to his ego when using Tom for impact. She named her vibrator *Tom* and held it up to him and said this made her feel better than his lovemaking…her trusty *Tom* and that resulted in a beating. Nina showed up at the studios the next day at her office, wearing no makeup or sunglasses, to allow everyone to see. Cameron was apologetic and oh so sweet post-assault, but she had a deadbolt placed on the bedroom door and threw all his clothes in the pool.

In her room she drank, and then to work, and then to home, and then to sleep. There were bottles of Bombay Gin and Stoli carefully tended in rows next to the wall. His side of the house became a man-cave and shooting gallery. Something had to give. When she walked through a plate glass sliding door, she was hospitalized and her parents placed her in the house in the hills.

"Nina, do you know why you're here?" The doctor asked.

She took a long puff on her cigarette and relaxed. "Yes, it's obvious that I wore out my welcome in the Emerald City."

Chapter Twenty

A simple message, "Hello." He stared at it a long time, and wondered what to do. He had no clue what her married name was, but he knew instantly it was her. Mary called in the middle of his revelry and his communication with her was disjointed, figuring she had caught him in the middle of something he was working out. She declared that she'd call him later, or see him at home.

Nina Kelly. He laughed, so she married a Mick after all. He knew all about what her parents referred to him as behind his back, but playing dumb all the same. Nina had spilled those beans long ago. She joked about what they'd say if she brought home a man named Goldberg or Rabinowitz. She went to school with both of those boys, and they lived in her neighborhood, part of her elementary school cadre and country club set. But even so, her father would twist into a pretzel knowing they were Jews.

Nina Kelly. So he went to her Facebook page and snooped around. There was the picture of her holding her son at what looked like a high school graduation and not much else as you had to 'friend' her to see other things. Her son looked like a very handsome lad and was much taller than mom. He attempted to study Nina's face, but the picture was smallish and she'd taken pains to make sure she was as undistinguishable as possible. He wondered about his own security settings and saw that his life was an open book with pictures and messages available to anyone that wanted to look. Damn!

So she probably saw his family and other pictures he put up. He wondered how weird it was for her to see all that. How weird was it just for him to know she had seen it. In the middle of that, Mary had called. He felt immediate guilt at hearing her voice as he stared at Nina's page. He was flustered, absent-minded, inattentive. He also had a coughing fit, and had been coughing a lot more lately. He hadn't smoked in years, but the cough and fatigue drove him to the doctors in the first place.

He decided on returning a simple message, "how dee-doo" to her, perhaps a brushstroke of his life since the 70's, and finally settled on "hello back." He couldn't for the life of him compose anything that didn't sound idiotic or puffy.

He hadn't thought of her in a long time and then when he did, he always wondered about things being different; if he hadn't been who he was, and what or who would he have been? Even saying that made him laugh. But he remembered about her uncanny way of stating something, or how she wrote and made such a succinct point. He had even tried to imitate her tight style of communication when writing papers. Once, when going through his boxes of former lives, he came upon some books she had dedicated to him. The pages yellowed and dog-eared; her tight and elegantly slanted cursive on certain pages explaining something. In that box he found his weathered copy of *The*

Little Prince she had given him. He held it a long time, thumbing through it, remembering the bookstore in Westwood where she had bought it.

They went there a lot when younger, and took buses everywhere, or were dropped off by her mother. Nina sat in the front seat while he was in the back, listening to her discuss things with her mother as if he weren't in the car. Her parents were like that, unengaged. He got used to it over the years, even though her father even warmed up to him a little when it looked as if he might be a prospective son-in-law. That was until the father asked what he wished to do in life. Tom answered, "Probably fix motorcycles." That had the effect of pissing on a small fire.

In that time, when he and Nina travelled by bus or parent, he was a wide-open boy. He never thought about a grown up future, or what he even wanted to do besides owning his own bike. He helped his older brother work on cars and bikes did odd jobs delivering papers, mowing lawns, cleaning out yards. He had saved money since the age of ten. Had his own bankbook and at fifteen had his eyes on a 650 Thunderbird at the BSA/Triumph dealership in Culver City. His brother had talked him out of a Victor 441 saying it was too small, and BSA's broke down too much. The Thunderbird needed work, but he was ready for it.

She enjoyed when they listened to records and she could explain a chord or something. There was a technique in picking a guitar called 'hammering' and she showed him knowing how to play and owning a beautiful acoustic Gibson she had him as her captive audience always. She had a collection of Dylan records that mirrored what he and his brother listened to and also Robert Johnson, who Tom had never heard of, but instantly became a blues aficionado after hearing his *Hellhound on My Trail*. When they listened to music and he wondered why the noises on the fret board were so distinguishable on *No Expectations,* she looked at him as if he were a lovable rube and explained it was the slide guitar mixed in the studio to stand out. You could hear Brian Jones's playing so clearly. It was as if for him, she was the font of all knowledge and merely had to tap into her to gain wisdom. How did she know all this shit?

To him, Nina was either a true genius or a borderline unit. She had a handle on everything. She had picked up guitar at six-years-old at a friend of her parent's, started strumming it. The owner of the guitar, a man who worked with her dad, showed her a few chords and she picked it up immediately. By fifteen she became bored with it. He couldn't blow a kazoo. But she played for him and showed him technique, and also how she open tuned her guitar and used a metal tube she got at the music store for a bottleneck effect. She played Johnson's *If I had Possession over Judgment Day* and *Stop Breaking Down Blues* and showed how she used the slide for punctuating and teasing it, making him just sit in wonder of her and ask what did she ever see in him?

She had always been precocious and intelligent and her parents had nourished that part of her too, but regretting not having total control when it came to her tastes in men when older. While Tom, who seemed a sweet boy and was cute, was definitely not a cut of the same cloth and was constantly the butt of her father's cultural humor. He was polite and admired and loved Nina immensely, but it was obvious to them he wasn't the sharpest tool in the shed.

Tom sat in his office at school, looking at his 'love me' wall and at an award he won for innovative educator of the year, and weirdly thought of Nina's dad, wishing he were there to see him get it. While being scared shitless of him when younger, he just wanted praise from him as he grew older. That Tom had eventually become an educator would have blown his mind, no doubt.

So many thoughts he had after seeing her 'hello' and then after sending his own back, he didn't know what to do. He felt excited and also frightened. Had he just opened a can of worms or had he opened a justified door to his past?

Nina logged on out of boredom and saw that she had a message notification. Tom.

"The game's afoot, Watson," she said to herself, smiling warmly.

Chapter Twenty-One

The idyll didn't last very long. The time apart had placed a translucent wedge in between them. Tom had troubles shaking his knowledge that someone else had lain with Nina, and she had regrets for her hasty reflexive need to see him after her donnybrook with Averill who called incessantly and she had had sex with him again, looting him of a few Quaaludes and a gram of coke, and finding in herself an unknown bit of Cruella Deville she didn't know existed within her. For Tom's part, he returned intermittently to the ballerina and Lauren, who had become quite surprising herself, somewhat in love with Tom.

There were good days and nights as well. They attended some local music venues like the Roxy and the Whisky to listen to music, and Nina having met many different people when in Averill's orbit got them backstage at a Bonnie Raitt concert at the Civic. She purchased an older BMW that was battleship gray and ran quite fast, so his bike fell by the wayside for most occasions, and Nina would come pick him up so he wouldn't be dressed like he was at Bike Week.

This phase of their affair found them seeing things in another light. They were older, looked more mature, and that teen look with rounded edges they had sported in the past was forever gone. Tom was filling out and had gained weight, not imitating a beanpole, while Nina had bloomed into total womanhood. No traces of anything baby on her anymore, the lines of her physique had transformed and seemed to invent a new and sylphlike air to her. Where people, both men and women alike, took note of her when younger, they now were obvious in their examinations.

Yet while they had taken on more adult personas, their relationship was static and hadn't moved forward locked in some strange teen angst. Tom was smarter, stronger, and more focused on his work and making some money; however, he was still reliant on her to be what she called 'the brains' behind it all.

She didn't like it anymore, and when with Averill, she didn't have to fight over intellect; Averill didn't have that insecurity, but she didn't wish to fall back into enabling Tom or opening his mind to a new author, film, or music. She couldn't see herself falling back into that again, being a teacher/mommy. His complacency in allowing her to say when or where annoyed her, but she was also gun-shy about wanting him to confront Averill or whoever, and her guilt at hurting him also deterring her from saying it out loud. Tom had fallen easily back into a pattern from before, and when not with her or at work, was busy with his other paramours. He hadn't been like this before and he was surprised when he found himself not feeling the least bit guilty when in another woman's' arms. He didn't understand why he kept at them sexually, when back in Nina's arms, but since that night in the motel, they had fallen back into an off and on sexuality that neither addressed, nor let go.

Lauren had asked him, if he wished to take a key. This amused him and upset him at the same time. He found himself just wishing to arrive, get horizontal, and then bid adieu, nothing more. She became a receptacle for him. And when she broached the idea of him having control over admittance, she became disposable, too. The key was the last thing he needed. On the nights he ventured out to her place, on the pretense of explaining to Nina that since they took her car everywhere he needed to ride once in a while, he didn't want any ownership of entry. He just wanted her there. And she was, since she barely went out at all, and then he wished to be gone. He couldn't process what he was doing or why, but was driven all the same. He blamed some of it on Nina, which alleviated some of his anger. His sex with Lauren increased in anger as well, and she accepted his rough handling of her and even acquiesce to what she felt were degrading acts. As his sexuality took an edge with Lauren and the ballerina, his sexuality for Nina waned, the vision of her and a faceless man fucking her would manifest and make him want to punch a wall...or fuck someone else.

Nina had been hired on at a small independent studio on Gower Avenue, and she was excited by the prospects. The news depressed Tom, and he saw them in two different worlds. Hollywood and Long Beach. Mars and Venus. It was a far haul from that night on the coast highway, when after he came back with some chips, candy, and a small pint of vodka to mix with orange juice, they had sex again. Slept on and off and talked the rest of the night about the future and the bounty of that vast unknown in front of them. They'd get a flat together, or a house maybe, they could do so many different things now that they were older, and she didn't have to worry about her parents. They were tired and yet excited. Looking back they knew it was so much smoke, but there were ties that bound them to each other, making them stand fast in a cement neither wished to admit or try to extricate themselves from.

The search for a place to live was half-hearted and tedious. To find a place that afforded a comfort zone for both and also splitting the difference between her work and his placed them in areas they didn't want to be. He would've preferred living closer to Manhattan or Redondo Beach to split the difference, but Nina wanted to live closer to Hollywood. The places they did look through were either in disrepair, had elevated rents, were contingent on the people living there moving out, and myriad issues such as sinks, drains, toilets, extra for a garage. Tom wondered if they could possibly move into the garage loft and co-habitat with her parents. Nina asked him if he had been lobotomized, as it was incredulous to her that he, of all people, wanted that proximity. It was indicative of his incentive to find a place for them.

Tom started reading some books she'd left out for him, and they had an effect he couldn't deny. He was reading Maugham's *The Razor's Edge* and after that Conrad's *Heart of Darkness*. Neither had any overlapping themes into his life, yet there were aspects to each that reached inside him, pulling him along as if he were an empty suitcase, being packed, and shoved out the door to go places. Different things motivated Tom and one was Maugham. He sought in himself any properties that he could share with Larry Darrell, and found himself wanting. He wanted to strive and develop a higher sense of self and perhaps even a spirituality that Darrell had as all others succumbed to the rat race and money. It was foolish in some ways, as times had changed and people just couldn't live that way. Even Larry and Isabel wouldn't have survived living in the way he wished, off the cuff and on the lark. In Marlow, he found his need to sail into something different. And Nina was firmly a creature of the concrete and needed someplace she could enjoy and cultivate as she lived in it.

There had always been an intrinsic complexity between Tom and outside forces affecting him. Like an animal knowing a storm was on its way and feeling that long shot of ozone in the atmosphere to warn it. For Tom, literature and people took on that affect. He knew what affect things or people had on him, yet wasn't always ready for his reaction. When he read *The Razor's Edge,* he saw in Larry an aesthetic man that he aspired to be. He felt as if the floor left him, without any footing or weight. His love for Nina wasn't grounding him anymore, and while in his heart he worshipped her in so many, many ways, she let him slip as if he had become separated from his anchor within her being, leaving him adrift. He couldn't even pretend to play house anymore in this state of feeling. He had to do something drastic and defining in his life. Nina seemed encased in her ambition and loved what she did; her idea of work always being writing of any form. He felt he was at a standstill and needed to recreate himself.

He had been working on receiving his merchant seaman card and moving out from yardbird to sailor. He hadn't told Nina, or anyone else for that matter. He was quietly packing things up at his dad's and aimed at putting his bike in a storage mode. But before doing that, he saw the ballerina once more, leaving teeth marks on her buttocks and Lauren, to just say goodbye. The thought of her sexually had passed for him and he didn't want to take that memory to sea with him in the future, so he just wished her the best. Anyway, it had been a long while since they had made love. He left her place astonished after she slapped him full on the side of his face and called him a chickenshit jackass. He hadn't expected that, but he took it, understanding why she might wish to do so. He smiled at her after the initial sting and shock wore off, but it still wasn't the memory he had wished to remember her by. He didn't think it in her. But was glad he discovered it, albeit too late.

When it seemed Nina was so firmly entrenched in her work, and her companions at the studio and she were inseparable, and he had inkling she was having an affair with a guy named Cameron, he made his decision and struck his plan and so now Nina knew what dry ice felt like on skin and it also felt like it was inside her, her anger was just that intense. And his fucking nerve. Yes, she was involved with Cameron, but so what? She was in love with *him*!

Chapter Twenty-Two

Some guy in the back apartment had freaked out after buying a bunch of records at a garage sale, and was trying with his trombone to play *Midnight in Moscow*. Tom was ready to vivisect him and his friends because they were obviously all trashed and drinking. He heard many times in a deep Samoan accented pidgin, "Suck 'em up, braddah!"

Mary looked at him as he tried to read a book for his classes, then said, "Eh…we need to move, Tom."

She had brought it up before, but he never took the bait, enjoying living so close to Kapiolani Park and downtown.

"You don't need to be *Townie*, Tommy…we can go windward, not like Kahuku, but just around the bend."

He nodded in agreement.

Mary's parents helped them buy a place in Kailua, a small house like 970 square feet near the canal, but for them it meant peace, quiet, and they could suck 'em up in peace if they needed to. Mary taught in Kai Muki while Tom, fully enrolled at UH, was working part-time at a bike repair place on Nimitz. They spent Fridays at clubs, Saturday at the beach surfing and killing hangovers, and Sunday in

Kahuku, eating, talking story with her family.

Their marriage had been at her parents' house with a huge party. His dad and brother declined to fly over, both having been absent from his life pretty much since he had shipped out thus rendering him an orphan and even more in need of Mary's family for support as they navigated this terrain, and they accepted him into their family. Miles enjoyed Tom's respect and also the help he gave in removing the junk cars from his yard. Mary was keen that the family liked him and also accepted by her multitude of cousins, aunties, and uncles. The plan was for him to obtain a teaching degree too and then maybe move off island in the future, renting their small bungalow in Kailua.

Every so often *she* would pop up in a conversation or mention of a book or film. Mary took the sting silently and absorbed it, knowing it wasn't meant to hurt, yet not being able to explain to him how much the pain sank deep into her after its initial hit. At times *her* presence just hovered like a spirit, some hurtful *aumakua* that needed a place to dwell and take a shape so she could keep it in check. She found a suitable stone way out leeward on the coast far past Waianae on the way to Kaena Point. It was large and oval like a pinecone and had many different holes in it from its voyage in the sea and time on shore, and she felt it was a suitable place for *her* spirit. Tom never noticed the stone sitting at the edge of the sofa on the floor closest to the sea.

Where a stone, long shaped by the sea and sands represented Nina, in California a small wristband that held her name, blood type and number of Next of Kin for emergencies represented her at the exact same time. Had Nina known her spirit was to be settled in a stone, she would have laughed at the irony and appreciated Mary's enshrining her thus. She was the last person to fear in Tom's life when she was resting at the house in the hills with all the other pampered drunks and users.

While there, she started playing guitar again and used it as a vehicle to take herself away. She played what she remembered, and then asked for some books to be brought in so she could learn other songs. She asked for and was approved to play in the Day Room and it was discovered that her playing was therapeutic for other people staying there with her. Her playing took her back to when she sat around and listen to records, playing by ear, recreating the sounds. She viewed it next to her predicament and believed that she should start playing by ear in the clinic she was in, recreating her life on some sort of semblance of sanity. And first things first were to jettison Cameron.

After his aborted 'rescue' attempt, he was arrested and brought up on charges of trespass, under the influence, and driving without a license. The restraining order violation was tossed as he was proven not to be within a hundred feet of the order, since Nina's place of residence was in the back. A stretch, granted, but his father knew the DA. Her contempt for him increased in kind with this peccadillo and she knew it was irrevocably broken.

She asked for more books than the library held and her knowledge impressed the staff. They discussed it as part of her therapy and then asked if she wished to be the in-house librarian. She viewed this with a somewhat jaundiced eye and let them explain it. She agreed and only because she could buy the books she wanted to and had to deem them necessary for others and why. This was an easy evil and so she did, and then giving a list to one of the house's caretakers, she awaited on her books.

Guitar, books, writing…it wasn't all so bad. Visits from her folks, haranguing her about the non-stop calls from Cameron, and hearing him whine into the phone was unnerving them. Nina offered them to stay in her room, eliciting not one laugh or smile. She knew how important this was to them and how much damage she had done. None of it was lost on her and she didn't discount their fears or embarrassment.

She, the golden one, had fucked up righteously. She wanted to tell them the irony of putting her in a place where most of the people needing help were using smack and coke daily, smuggled in by loved ones and friends. The posh grounds and well-coiffed vegetation and beautifully addressed rooms housed some of the biggest active dope fiends in Los Angeles. One guy stayed there regularly just to get his family off his back and had offered her all of it. They snuck off to grab a quick cigarette when he broached the idea of her sleeping with him for some dope. She had to laugh at that one…being in this place because her husband was a dope fiend and she a doper *and* drunk, and then meeting the doppelganger of her husband inside. She was determined to not repeat her mistakes and decided to make a move to get assistance in leaving. She'd had enough and didn't feel like she needed a 12-step program for that. She needed to get away from the dope fiends and drunks inside! One guy, really very crazy, always asked her to listen to accordion music in his room. He combed his hair like Dick Contino and drove her to distraction. It was time to go.

Chapter Twenty-Three

She had been out of rehab some time when she and Art did get serious. He was thriving in his business, had finally repaired the Porsche to his liking, sporting a nice clean coat of German racing silver. He liked Nina a lot, still scorched by his first vision of her. He knew she had been through a rough patch and after her wings melted, crashed back to an earth that didn't allow a soft landing. He didn't know that much about post-alcoholic problems, but he read up on them and even attended a couple of AA meetings with her when she felt in the mood, then shook her head in disgust as to why she even bothered.

"The stories bring me down. The First Step, "surrender", is always a rough gig. They lay it out, the whole history, and some of it starts early, like before their teens. It's depressing." They went out, and she insisted he still drink around her and not let her life rule him. But, if they kissed later, he had to chew gum or gargle. He would.

"That night in the Raincheck Room…I really was quite taken by your looks. I knew men were looking at you when you walked in with Corinne. Sorry, but they can't have been looking at her."

"You're so mean, Art. She and I have known each other a long time. You just don't give a friend like that the boot because she looks like that." Art would smile when he stuck pins in Corinne. He and Nina were on the verge of sleeping together, but he knew she was hesitant after her problems, didn't want to jump into something right way. He had patience after his own divorce, almost drowning in that and swimming back to shore, barely alive. He only read maybe three of the books she recommended and couldn't tell a Matisse from R. Crumb, but she knew he was genuinely interested and trying on many different levels to connect.

For Art, she was some rare and beautiful moment he stumbled upon serendipitously, just wishing to have a well-made drink and listen to a great jukebox. When seeing her across the room, he felt as he had when he first had feelings for a girl in grade school class, this confusing rush of pleasure and no idea of how to deal with it. He had to strap on his swagger and just go for it when she came over in his direction. When he caught her Bardot smile, he had to blink and regain his footing. He felt as though he'd stumbled and fallen to the floor as if his cane had been kicked out from beneath him. He thought that sort of feeling was bullshit, but he swore he could bear witness after that.

Art pretty much prescribed to the idea that if you married your high school sweetheart and walked the straight and true, it'd be okay. His own parents married before the war and were still together, come hell, high water and even Vatican II. He lived in that vacuum so long and working at making it work, he hadn't noticed she wasn't even his wife anymore. Dressing for the other man, wearing her hair for him. And when the lights finally came on, he was caught flat-footed, his head an all-day sucker. He was a tourist in his own home, and the vacation was done. And then he had to pay for her fucking someone else because of the kids. There were no Gods left for men, he was convinced. Seeing Nina, her thick corn silk hair catching the ceiling lights, making it shimmer when she walked in. Those mocking deities had returned him a favor, a solid. And he had to laugh at the excitement he was experiencing. It takes a lot to make a man laugh out of nowhere, he mused.

So he hung with her, not realizing how intellectually flat-footed he was as well. How did men keep up with her? Whatever it took, he was there. He lay in his bed and listened to John Kay's *Easy Evil* while he smoked, and all he could do was think of her. It was a far cry from the Jimmie Rodgers and Johnny Mathis he and his ex listened to. Nina was, for him, a sensuous sin. He played it over and over again; convincing himself he wasn't OCD, just in love.

Nina was temporarily staying at her parents while her flat was being painted, and they talked a lot on the phone, conversing on the same pink Princess she did with Tom when they first started sparking at fourteen. How weird was that she thought! She remembered laying across her bed, then turning over, her head over the side, running her fingers through her thick hair to the ends, then inspecting them to see if they were brittle, then stretching her legs straight up and turning the other way, like a constellation moving across the sky, her little body in movement as she and Tom spoke, their voices making them squirm and spin in the confines of their rooms like pure energy, and not ever wishing to hang up. Now she was talking to Art, for what seemed centuries away from that time, sitting in an easy chair with her leg thrown over the side, an ashtray in her lap and blowing smoke at the ceiling. When first she went home and was back in her old room, she saw the phone and wanted to laugh at how insanely dated it was, a part of her personal Smithsonian Kit. Artifacts from her childhood and teen years that have since gone extinct. There were even some LPs tucked in under the bed she discovered. The Stones *Aftermath* was on the top, below that *Surrealistic Pillow*. How many times had she and Tom listened to *that* figuring out Jagger's lyrics on *Goin' Home*, and making out like mad when her parents stepped out, her bra pulled up to her neck? There was a whole stack of stuff stashed under there. That was back when they took the bus to Wallach's Music City on Sunset and Vine, listening to all the new albums that came out in the small little soundproof booths. Womanhood, she smiled dryly, isn't all that it's cracked up to be.

So she chatted with Art as she waited out the three days the painting and refinishing took, her landlord insisting it happen *now*. She made different discoveries of various items and realized her mother probably hadn't even vacuumed in there for the years she'd been gone, a shrine to her daughter. Then Art asked if she wanted to stay at his place for the night, drive up to the Raincheck, meet and then he'd drive her up into Laurel Canyon to what he laughingly called his lair. She was ready and game. She needed a man right now and had succumbed to his charm and stamina. How any man could put up with her was a mystery, and she gave him props for hanging in there with her. It was time to see what this was all about.

Chapter Twenty-Four

What to write? Was he obligated to write back? What could he possibly say that doesn't sound totally lame? Did he care if he was…and if so, why? The questions.

He tried to couch in many ways that he was happy, had a beautiful son and wife, and while life wasn't so much fun now after visiting a doctor, he couldn't complain, and he thought of her on and off. No. Well, it's been a very long time and I hope you're well. Maybe. I'm glad to see you're doing okay and I like that picture of you at your son's graduation. Closer. Is that your son? Lame.

He just couldn't spit anything out that was simple, yet to the point that he could accept.

Then, he just typed in blindly, "Are you going to the reunion?" And he sent it off. After he did, he felt like the angry man who after the words exited his mouth wished his fingers could retrieve them and place them back inside. He felt like a ninny. But that was it, and he had sent it out. He'd been guilty of that in the past with her. Saying things in an explosive moment that he wanted to retrieve. His hair trigger moments when his mother, having passed when he was very young was brought up, and his father having a woman come in twice a week to do laundry, kitchen cleaning, and all around "womanly" things he hadn't a handle on magnifying the inept house in which he was being raised.

There were the times he was jealous over stupid things, unreal things, and let slip from his tongue the most ridiculous words. If Nina gushed over some record or book, in his mind he'd target the author or singer or guitarist with jealous crosshairs. Nina wanted to see the Stones at the Forum really bad in '69 and he was jealous of Jagger. Thinking back on that now, he felt like a total idiot and wondered what she saw in him to put up with his petty rages. They weathered both their jealousies from her dislike of raceways and bike shops to his waiting for her in a boutique while she tried on fifty things. Or they dug around in thrift stores and second hands for some treasure in the form of an ancient aloha shirt or a Dale Evans snap button style for women from the 50's or perhaps a beret or a stylish hair clip from somewhere in Silverlake or Venice. They had petty jealousies that they tolerated and tabled and then some that burrowed to the surface, and when free of being incarcerated, screamed loudly and had ugly consequences. He wouldn't talk about women around Nina, if he felt a woman was quite beautiful or striking, and he would only be passive and agree with her if she felt a woman was glamorous or unique looking. Old movie stars were safe, because most were either dead or getting there, so his longtime crush on Marlene Dietrich meant nothing, but he felt if he mentioned that he thought Tina Turner or Marianne Faithfull hot, he'd get into trouble. So he kept his own counsel while Nina spoke her mind.

There was always that difference in that he felt he was in some way protecting her ego and feelings about herself if stayed quiet, while accepting her honesty in voicing her opinion. He knew if she mentioned Warren Beatty that way, it didn't mean he was going to be doing her next week, but his hackles went up all the same. He felt that idiotic feeling again, as a teen when he sent that message out. So he sat there at his desk with a video on in his mind of all his poor moments of anger, wishing he had just shut the hell up.

It was never that way with Mary. Was it maturity? When did he mature? He remembered getting pissed once when surfing, shortly after they were married on O'ahu. Some local guys were talking to her on the beach about her board, made by a local board maker, as he came out of the surf. He was jealous of them. No matter what, he was still an outsider. So he came up to her and said 'let's go' while she was still talking and walked by her. When she caught up with him, he was already regretful at being an ass, and apologized. She told him he owed a favor to her because they all wanted to kick his white ass. He didn't mind doing her favors anyway, as most resulted in his hair being pulled this way and that. But it faded out in him, the heat from his teens and early twenties.

He tried to recall a time in the near past he had been so stupid as to wish his words were taken back, but he couldn't. Mary had a settling effect on him that he couldn't explain, but it basically had to do with her temperament. Her even keel and pragmatism kept him on course once he set out on his academic adventure at UH. Her composure, even under pressure, was schooling him as much as seeing a putt in your line, knowing the breaks beforehand. She drained him of the anger he carried, while dormant most of the time, had its moments of ferocity. At times, he'd been so verbally brutal in the past, his past life as he referred to it now, that just the mention of it was embarrassing and rendered him lethargic.

Nina too said things to Tom she'd never dream of saying to Art, knowing full well that even though Art held her aloft in his view of her, she owned Tom in many ways and could say things he wouldn't rejoin, while Art would either give it back in spades or laugh at her. When she read Tom's reply, she laughed at the brevity and the directness of it. Well, she thought, he has changed a lot! The old Tom would have beat around the bush, fishing for words, and her loving him for being at times a bumpkin. Who was this bold man of few words she had unleashed? She wrote him back:

"Maybe." *Your move.*

Chapter Twenty-Five

It was a warmer than usual day and he felt like a beer, so decided to hit up the Giant store on the way home from work. He was a few days off his oncology appointment and decision making time, so a beer sounded very nice. He wasn't even hungry and thought perhaps this was part of the process he was going through, lack of appetite, among other things. He'd fallen into a trough and decided to just ride out that wave current and let himself go with it. There could be worse things, like his rectum falling out as he walked down the street.

In the store, he found the six-pack of Longboard, imported from Hawaii, and he couldn't help himself from shouting as loud as he could in his mind, "Suck em up, braddah!" He loved the lager taste and the design of Diamond Head on the bottle. It brought so much back. He smiled, the secret little crumpling of his lips that only Mary knew. Mary. He was standing in the checkout line and a woman was in front of him in a spaghetti strap summer dress, fitting for the unexpected temperatures. The exposed skin of her shoulders were presented to him, and as he was at least a half a foot taller, took it all in, over her shoulders, and the swell of her bust. Her flesh, having hid all winter until now was very white, and against the yellow material looked like mayonnaise. And for a passing second, he wondered what it felt like, but a wave of nausea crept over him. He thought perhaps he was sick, but he wasn't. It was Mary. She was so deep inside him, he being so infused with her that seeing this woman's skin and imagining touching or feeling it upset him. Mary's scent, her skin texture, hair…how abundant and wild it was when she wasn't pinning it down and sweeping it back, French braiding its length; bringing Hawaii back to his senses. What she felt like next to him in bed, or when gone for some seminar or something that being the principal of a school had her doing, how empty and desolate her side of the bed was. He would, if she were gone a day or two, place laundry he had folded on her side of the bed to give it relief as if someone were there. Or he'd use her pillow instead of his to have her scent there for him, faded perfumes or shampoo smells. She wore one of his old tees to bed or his heavy blue pajama top when he wore the bottoms. He was startled at the reaction he felt in looking at this woman's skin and how almost violently his senses retreated into Mary, and all the real estate she had inside him. She moved into almost every space he had inside, commandeering all his senses. Her hold on him wasn't the death grip that some wives maintain, it was a more an ethereal embodiment that like a fine smoke gained access to all his pores and saturated him.

He recalled moments in the past when she was on top of him, her hair hanging and forming a canopy just like they were inside, and she'd grind on him and whisper for him to marinate in her. It was his and he could just use it how he wished. Her silhouette, an *akua*, and supernatural above him, and he felt as if he were out of his body. The woman's shoulder was an insult to his thoughts, and for a second an outrage enveloped him having to see it juxtaposed against his memory of Mary, naked above him.

Nina had expressed the idea of human real estate and love to him long ago, as they hung together, at the old deco hotel in Santa Monica, their room *makai,* facing the ocean, a large moon creating a small stream on the placid night surf. They were on the floor below the penthouse and had a spectacular view, the room forgotten, empty bottles, and leftover Chinese with cigarettes put out in the pint containers. She told him about letting him inside of her and how much room she had for him that he didn't even realize yet. But she also warned that she wouldn't give it all to him, that there were vast stretches inside her no one could or should claim. She refused to give it all up, and then she laughed and poked him when she said most of it was prime property.

He felt somewhat hurt when she said that. While she was explaining her inner real estate ideas to him he was already telling himself simultaneously that he'd give her all of him. Every bit he had inside was hers, and he was willing to do that, so willing. Her declaration of keeping some areas inside her private made him feel again, he was giving too much of himself away, and he was being foolish in that thinking. They had these discussions post lovemaking as Nina felt expansive at these times and relaxed, her world flat-lined happily with no pressures or stress. Nude, she'd sit up in the bed, cross-legged, or like then, in the room, sitting in the room chair pulled up to the window, her feet up on the sill, a cigarette between two fingers waving about like a small conductors baton, Tom her orchestra.

Mary…he had let her inside and allowed her almost everything. She was so a part of him, even thinking of other women turned him off. But Nina's memory burned somewhere in there, like a buried ember, tiny and lost under so much ash, yet still displaying a faint glow, filled with an almost imperceptible heat; fading but not yet dead. He couldn't even remember most names or faces of the women in between or during his times with Nina and before Mary, but her spark survived, and he felt guilt. But if he thought of her, he didn't feel the queasiness he did when he looked upon that woman's shoulder in the market. Nina still had a firm grip someplace inside him, some dell or meadow of his consciousness that he couldn't detect whatever compass used or azimuth he shot. It was how he thought of her as he floated between both women, admiring both simultaneously, yet separately. He was convinced he wasn't alone in this, that he wasn't the only man who harbored a secret thread of communication to his past that he used for a surreptitious look back. Then again, maybe he was, and he felt flawed and anemic.

He wondered how much of him was left in Nina's real estate. Had she sold the memory of his house or was it boarded up, dilapidated in some dark place she never ventured? What was left of him? He knew, maybe just his ego desired it, to have a place in her mind, some small vestibule of her heart that he dwelled in. It meant nothing really, but he wished it all the same. She broke the thick sheet of ice that laid over their collective love for over thirty years; old, ancient ice, blue as the sky. She had cracked it open with one, *hello*.

He had to be in there somewhere.

Tom spent the evening drinking his beer and working in his garage, reconstructing the 750 Trident that had become his solid bridge to the past.

Chapter Twenty-Six

"You look like I remember you, behind a bike and happy. I hope things have gone well for you. I'm still in L.A., Brentwood (no, not near the OJ murders) and am happily married and have a son in college. I see you have a son, too."

Then two hours later. "Oh yea, I forgot, yes, I am going to the reunion."

Tom just stared at the message, and then erased them fast as if someone were looking over his shoulder. Damn. He wrote back tepidly:

"That's great. I am very happy. I am going to the reunion, probably hanging out with Will, if he gets his plastic surgery in time."

Again after he sent it he had a WTF come-to-Jesus moment. She sounded the same, same humor in that bit about living in Brentwood. She must have done well, or her husband and she both doing well. His replies sounded as if he were Ozzie's neighbor, Thorny.

He wrote back to her after a long deliberation, "Hey Nina, I'm glad you sent me a message and we can see each other at the end of April. We have a lot of catching up to do. I have thought of you on and off through the years and always hoped things would be good for you."

And that was that. He sent off an e-mail to Will letting him know when he was going to fly into L.A., since Will, at times, had an aversion to memory. Then he added "…and Nina is going to be there." He stretched out in his chair, again looking out the window overlooking the walkway, his yard, and driveway. Mary was swimming and he started to his garage to work on the electrical system of the bike. He scored a great manual and schematic at a flea market where a guy had bike parts, pictures, posters, and parts for all manner of bikes, but then stopped and went up to his office room above the garage and read his messages and sent his e-mail.

He deliberated over whether or not to work on the bike, and then drifted off into web surfing. He looked at bikes, rallies, Triumph clubs in the mid-Atlantic region, and finally his high school website and entered himself into the system there as an alumni. He cruised through some of the pictures from other classes and then on his own, people posting up pre-reunion. Many of the guys had what he laughingly termed a 'five-head' as their hair had receded revealing more skin, increasing the 'fore-head'. There were jowls, baldness, died hair, long hair, pulled back hair, and comb-overs. There were obviously reconstructed faces and breasts, many more in glasses and a few that looked like Nick Nolte's mug shot or the horn rimmed glasses of 'The Far Side.' He included his faculty picture, suit lapels and tie, smiling into the camera. In his profile he listed Mary Lani Totave Kelleher as his wife and Drew Kohanomoku Kelleher as his son. In the pictures he looked at, he didn't see all of his classmates and wondered how many were already dead besides the ones he had found out about through Will, who lived on Face Book and kept his finger on the happenings from school. He saw a few he wished to never see again and a couple of the women he had random thoughts about while tethered to Nina. He always thought he might ask some others out if he hadn't been with Nina. But they were together since junior high, and other people in their class knew it, and if there were some secret thoughts directed at him, they'd never seen the light of day for him. He found the Shreft brothers, of whom he despised both, one a skinny prevaricating turd and the other a pudgy ass who felt you needed to give him respect even when his jockey shorts were exposing his crack when he bent over. Tom started remembering all the people he went through school with and then realized he saw them all through the combined lens of him and Nina both. He couldn't remember a person they had *not* talked of, or dished outright. Of course he had one on one dealings with them all, people in his classes or in sports, social events, but Nina had been so much a part of his opinionating. He defaulted right back into what they both conceived for whatever person he saw or thought of. He felt as if he was blind and she was describing the world around to him.

He didn't resent it, but thought it as a phenomenon of sorts in the academic sense of the word, and not the circus definition. She had been his eyes and helped him to define in his own mind, each person in their classes or social circle. He gave up that to her and it was only now that he saw and understood it. No one came out to his face and told him he was whipped, but when he went to piss during this epiphany, he gazed into the mirror and admitted to himself and the surrounding men's room, "I was whipped." He was a blank slate, the little green ball of clay, the accouterment to her strength and force when they were in school. He wondered if everyone saw him that way too, her accessory. What could he do now? Ruefully, he thought of that song he loved as a kid, *Cathy's Clown* and wondered if he had been Nina's clown. If so, he wore it well then and seemed not to have lost sleep over it.

Nina always considered Tom as a kindred soul who saw things how she had them framed and agreed. They were simpatico. In school, even from a young age, she always felt a nagging insecurity under what looked like a confident face, almost what one considered a swagger for a child. Her closest friends were the boys in class, thinking the girls didn't accept her for who she was, even in grade school. They felt little girls around her, as if they were in the company of an adult and it was uneasy for them. Nina's looks set her apart and it was easy to look at her and picture her as an adult. Where the other girls looked as if they'd go through some cosmic metamorphosis, Nina looked like a miniature adult, even at a young age having sexuality about her. Her mother identified this and made sure that she downplayed Nina's difference by dressing her down, not helping to accentuate her face and body.

By junior high school, Nina started choosing her own clothes, and much to her mother's chagrin, was attracted only to the clothes her mother had avoided buying for her when younger. The 60's were in full swing and miniskirts and boots were the rage. Nina wore her thick blonde hair like Marianne Faithfull, after seeing her on *Shindig* singing, *As Tears Go By*. She loved Faithfull's back-story, having her mother a Sacher-Masoch, whose great-great uncle wrote the scandalous *Venus in Furs* and she was sleeping with Mick Jagger. Nina felt a connection to the Stones and Marianne and loved Tom more for the fact that he too listened to almost nothing but the Stones and his beloved Link Wray. She understood what the feeling was behind music and could infer things others her age had no clue about; her own sexuality filling her and the music being a strange and melodic release when she played guitar. Her selection gravitated to music that was filled with some sensuality or another. The graphic and double entendre laden blues or the seething misogyny of *Aftermath* gave her a release as well as the harmonious folk singers, like the urgency in Donovan's *Oh Deed I Do* or the hypnotic stupor of Dylan's *Sad Eyed Lady of the Lowlands*. When she first started looking at Tom in school during the one class they shared and explored what this tall boy with raven black hair did to her, she played at home and thought of him next to her, nude. The two entwined like vipers in a nest. She thought of him for months before sending out the note through her friend, Naomi, to ask him what he thought of her. The note that changed both of their lives. At night in her room, alone and listening to the radio or her stereo on low, she fancied moments with him in her fantasies. This different boy in jeans and Elvis hair, so unlike her grade school boys who were being groomed for prep schools or junior entry level jobs at their father's firms or businesses. She knew all about those boys, but she didn't know about this one. She found herself making sure they crossed paths even when not in the same class so she could see more of him, or find him hanging out at recess and lunchtimes to study him. His Levis faded to almost a bluish white, his high top Chuck Taylor's as faded as his jeans and his tee shirts accentuating his long sinewy frame. Sometimes he was invisible at lunch and she thought he was ditching, and then discovered he was in the shop classes hanging out with the drafting teacher, drawing motorcycles in blow apart diagrams. That also intrigued her. His notebook didn't advertise any girls or sport teams like most boys' did. Tom's had a huge, oval Triumph logo, and nothing else. Was this competition she'd have to compete against?

At night, it was Tom that brought her to orgasm, as she put towels across the bottom of her door to soak up any noises she made while hiding under blankets, her night gown around her waist. She kissed him, held him, smelled him, tasted him…her only reference some lewd Aubrey Beardsley drawings of huge phalluses bestowed on his thin frame. She wanted him, at fourteen, and wanted him now. In their shared class, she sat behind him in the next aisle over and watched his back, right arm, and head from her vantage point. She found herself yearning for that arm to be around her, her hand holding that thick mesh of black, inky hair, pulling him down to her lips. And now, some forty-four years north of fourteen, she was a bit blown away that she felt that same urge again.

Chapter Twenty-Seven

Mary thought a while about what was up with Tom lately. He didn't seem as robust or as active as he used to be. He didn't go in for workouts, but was a busy person in that he was always moving, shark-like through his life and had his hand on something. Lately though, it seemed as if he was under a weight, and that wasn't the man she knew. The sex that had happened spontaneously a while back had been good, and she never felt as if she lost something if he wasn't entirely erect for the time they were together. It was the intimacy that she coveted and loved so much. When she looked at him, she saw the shock of white hair that she saw happen in stages, until it looked like new snow. But she still saw it as if it were super imposed on him, that black-haired man at the beach that day, walking in Kapiolani, the one she flirted with in that capricious moment. That never changed. But things weren't right in her realm, and he was definitely off kilter. That worried her. Her first thought was maybe another woman, but his script for his ED pills was at the same level almost forever. Then thinking he had a separate script, she checked on the script number at the pharmacy to see if another had been given. No, it wasn't another script, so it was something else. She knew this man…then asked herself, *Do I?*

She thought so.

She'd never known him to be hesitant in doing something; he was always resolute from start to finish in whatever he set out on. When they lived near the park on Collins, in the beginning, and she said it was time for him to lead, follow, or get the heck out of the way, he enrolled and finished ahead of schedule, and got his certificate to teach and he did so in Hawaii Kai. By that time, she was at Castle High as an assistant VP, working on her Masters, fast tracking in her career. And Tom hadn't disappointed her in his resolve.

When they bought their cottage in Kailua, their *Menehune* house as they called it because it was small enough for the Night Marchers to all fit in, life was work, surfing, seeing her family, and taking exuberant rides over the Pali on Sunday mornings on his bike. They'd hit some little tourist place for the cheap kine breakfast on Kuhio, hanging with the late night people who were finishing whatever sketchy business, and eating before disappearing into the sunlit dawn. Or they hit Kelly's on Nimitz, and get beer with their eggs, watching the sailors from Pearl and their escorts trying to sober up. She missed those mornings all of a sudden and wished that bike in the garage was done and they could jump on it and find some out of the way place to stop and snuggle at as they ate.

Was her husband slipping away? Next to her diamond that he finally bought after he sold the Triumph, she still wore the first ring he gave her that night of the graduation party, her sweetheart ring, *Kuuipo* faded and worn, yet still legible. Like a larger than expected wave that hits one at the beach, knocking them over as it captures them in its tumult, she felt off balance and legless and in that second longed for O'ahu. Longed for that time she and Tom shared, conceived Drew, and planted plumeria trees in the yard wondering how large they were now some twenty-five years later.

She went into his office and moved the cursor, revealing the screen; news and weather. She looked at his favorite sites and saw a plethora of motorcycle websites, parts, gear, clothing. There were some educational blogs and some political ones and one curious one about the Polonio Pass in California's south central valley. She clicked on his history by date and saw that he'd been on Face Book. His reunion had set up a page of and he had visited it, surfing through the pictures. Was it the impending reunion that he was distant about?

She had decided not to attend her 30th reunion. For one thing, her work schedule didn't allow for it, and another, she just had no connection to her high school friends. She knew most still lived island and had probably settled into their parents' houses, now the old ones in the in-law suites, or gone. Her dad was gone now, and her mother enjoyed when Drew and his school chums surfed North Shore and stopped in, starving and they all brought life and laughter back into the house. Many moved becoming Townies, starting new roots Leeward in the houses that were pushing up like mushrooms from Waipahu to Waianae. She had bumped into one girl she had attended school with and couldn't count the Hawaiian heritage bracelets she wore or layers of lacquered nail polish. She didn't fit in there anymore after she and Tom moved east, chasing better jobs and settling in a house, if on island, would cost four times what they paid in Maryland. Should she push him and ask to attend his reunion with him?

No.

Chapter Twenty-Eight

Nina started back to work and was doing well. She and Art were married, and while they didn't talk kids right away, it was the question in the room unanswered. The elephant in the room, so to speak. There was something deep within Nina that had her hesitating when it came to procreation. Would she relapse? Was it fair to the kid? Art had kids and she enjoyed hanging with them when his visitation allowed. Happily, his wife had remarried, Art explaining it that she must have changed her shorts and re-baited her hook. Nina only smiled and shook her head, having a similar view of her own ex.

Cameron had bottomed out, and over the years slipped in and out of rehab like a snake in a frying pan. His addiction took him into south central Los Angeles and he was beaten severely by locals who took umbrage to white people in Mercedes coming into their neighborhoods to buy smack. She never returned a call he made, but he called on and off until she used the technology at hand and blocked his calls. But her own kid…that was a thing she thought of each time she and Art made love. She cursed herself and was angry. She read so much literature about the biological clock, as each time she felt Art deep in her she felt the ticking of her clock, as if she were the crocodile in search of Hook.

She took her BC pills religiously and made sure she had no health issues. Her visit to rehab was a reminder of how hubris and folly, when co-mingled, caused serious problems. The memory of her stay at the bar window house was almost comical for how useless it was, still making her shiver.

Art worshipped her and she returned his love easily. Since meeting him, she was secure and well inside. There was a over a decade between them in age and she considered this as something she needed, an older man who had maturity, had lived in his skin and still enjoyed it and loved her unconditionally. Cameron had been too much like the boys she grew up with who had privilege and were groomed to shit on other people and not really losing sleep over it. Their nuptials were doomed from the beginning, she saw in hindsight, knowing full well her marriage to him was a reaction to her father's disgust over Cameron, even calling him a pansy to her face. He declared that even Tom had bowling sized balls in comparison, to which she remarked, "If I had married Tom, he wouldn't have measured up either. In the end, he'd just be another plain, shanty Irish."

Her father's silence cemented that.

But Art, he was so different from what she knew in her past that they meshed well and she enjoyed his company. Her father, being a just a decade older than Art, enjoyed having conversations with him and enjoyed watching sports or golf when they came over on Sundays when Art didn't have his kids. She made him trade the Porsche in and get an old ragtop Benz, and made him take her out the coast highway at night. She'd un-tether her hair and let it blow wild, a shock of blonde, white whips and it excited him to look over at her as she put her head back, enjoying the wind, letting it take her hair and caress or push on her face, her arm outside, a cigarette in her hand, the burning end almost extinct in the speed of the car. Once they pulled up into one of the canyon roads, found a pull off and she straddled him, wearing a skirt on purpose, wanting him. Art had stopped drinking as they made their life together. He missed it at first and then it was a distant memory, like a school friend he was close to, but lost contact with over the years. Feeling some memory of attachment and certain things and times spent when seeing a dog-eared picture from that past, but not wishing to reconnect. Nina silently thanked him in different ways, not wishing to speak the obvious, but leaving small gifts or physical tokens of her feeling for him.

Her first pregnancy caused a cyclone of buried fears to swirl about her and started to destroy her *wa*, her harmony. She had had breakfast, and then when reading over a manuscript and lighting a cigarette she felt nauseas. Maybe it was the coffee and smoke she was consuming and wondered what she had eaten the day before that perhaps brought it on. The next morning she awoke feeling as if she could hurl across the room. When Art asked if she were okay, she answered with her "hurl across the room" feeling.

Art joked around that she should drop by Thrifty's and get a pregnancy test. She scolded him and asked to kindly shut the fuck up. When she left for the day, her first stop was the Thrifty's down the street on Wilshire.

She was pregnant. Her next stop was to buy a fifth of vodka. When Art came home, he saw her car pulled diagonally across the drive. Inside the house, she was trashed and half dressed in the kitchen, the bottle empty and another that wasn't on its side almost half full. There were cigarette burns on the island in the kitchen and cold ash scattered on the floor. Nina was speaking in some unknown and strange tongue, one of the words he thought he made out, as he asked her slowly and in a fragile voice what had happened, was, *baby*. He called her parents, called UCLA, and then hauled ass to the emergency room with Nina strapped in next to him, throwing up in the Benz. That was the first time. Post-stomach pumping, she managed to escape again, when her mother napped at her home while overlooking the damages. They found her over a week later

Here comes your nineteenth nervous breakdown.

Nina couldn't get it out of her head, and then just stopped and let it play on. She was in a quiet room now, and her mattress didn't have a sheet, she wore pajamas that were peculiar in they seemed to be of one piece so as not to be able to take off. She figured they were peeking into the small rectangular window Q15 minutes to make sure she wasn't either eating her mattress or hanging from the rafters. She might have yelled, "Here it comes!" a few times herself, but wasn't sure.

She knew she was on something and couldn't figure out if it was Valium or Librium. She giggled, thinking Valium would have helped this bash, riffing on Lou Reed, since she wasn't going anywhere. Had she mentioned to Art, if she hadn't killed him, that she was pregnant? Maybe she shouldn't be on any meds now. One random thought entered her mind about Tom seeing her like this. Her Conradian sailor, Marlow, now up a river. She'd been awake too long, she figured, and closed her eyes to sleep. Later, when they decided she wasn't harmful to herself and ingesting clear fluids, she was allowed to have a sheet and a blanket. She asked the nurse to inform her husband and the doctor that she was pregnant and to make some decisions for her. She then took a very long and restful sleep, wondering before she drifted off what the future held for her. She didn't hear the song anymore after that.

Chapter Twenty-Nine

In his garage, he worked on the bike. He also looked back on his ongoing dialogue with Nina. He used his work e-mail because he was paranoid of using Face Book, and he felt better to be able to relate his life, over the last thirty odd years to her. It was almost surreal to hear about what she had done, and also that she had issues with alcoholism. He tried picturing it, yet he couldn't. She updated his mental filing cabinet, sending him pictures and updates of her life, and her son Alexander, who looked striking with his bowl of blonde white hair, so much Nina.

He'd write her, feeling as if he needed to make some amends here and there, or explain himself, but he deleted the passage in seconds that took painstaking minutes to compose. He could almost feel the hesitancy in her letters as well, when they discussed something from the past, a time when she felt she acted poorly to him or slighted him, and he addressed it from his end. They danced around this campfire of regret and missed opportunities in each missive. They wrote things that the one hopes the other wasn't drinking coffee while reading, opening a flood of old forgotten sayings, humor, faces made, instances of hilarity, or deep embarrassment. They dished up old friends and classmates and teachers. They added up their dead and living and silently held their own counsel on each one mentioned. They talked about their kids and the obvious joy and pride they took in parenting. Nina mentioned her being the uber-mother and her husband, Art, always having to intervene and inject what he called 'man sauce' into the mix. Tom had to laugh, remembering the same when Mary was too much the overprotective mom. Waves her family used to let her play in were too big for her *keiki*! He had to laugh seeing what size waves she surfed as a twelve-year-old.

So when they went to Sandy's or Maka Pu'u, he accompanied Drew into the water. Kailua State Beach was like a lake, so they only went there to swim. Nina and her crew did snowboarding and ski trips in the season.

It was so weird to be talking like this after so many years. It brought back silent and vivid memories that had long been undisturbed. He recalled moments of extreme pleasure and also pain. He never told her he had staked out the gallery where she worked part-time for Averill, and saw him with other women when she wasn't there, and his attraction to other men as well when she wasn't around, which was obvious even to Tom. He never would either. How real his memories were, once they shed the caskets they were shunted into, and over time, embalmed in the overlap of more memories until totally submerged in some backwater of his head. Now, at times, they were vibrant and loud, while still others were flashlights in that primeval bog, barely discernible.

Nina felt almost identical to Tom in mirroring his thoughts

concerning their reconnection. It was so odd. She thought of things or clothes she wore, not ever giving any thought to remembering something so trivial, but Tom filled in the blanks and gave her a complete picture of her in space and time. They had never broke the thin connecting wire between them that had lain dormant for so long; no voice or sound crackling over it in so many years. Now she felt good reading his words and laughing at something he would remember or bring up. She also hid the fear of her attraction to him … still. She felt a tingle when she was alone after reading a message and find herself wet. She looked in the mirror after writing him back and forth, and surveyed herself. She held this woman, this image against those days. She wanted him to think her attractive, to still know she had the allure. Then she'd feel silly afterwards and vainglorious.

She remembered the time he left her to go to sea, as they disintegrated, attempting to reconcile, the two of them still not knowing how to set up their own house or be responsible to another person. God, if only we were older then and knew more, she had sighed. She accused him of apostasy in leaving her! Then she stared in the mirror again and wondered what he'd say about this woman who stood in the fire, burning through a couple of lives in her time? Would he admire this woman, she wondered, or would he not? She burned off her outer skin and had in its place a flesh chainmail of hardness from what she'd done to her body. She winced, knowing she killed her baby following the episode at UCLA, and her subsequent Mr. Toad's Ride. Art, almost clean of his sanity, himself a tree that all the live bark was stripped off.

She didn't confess to Tom of that shameful chapter during which she also cheated and ran afoul of the law. She torched the castle like mad villagers in a *Frankenstein* movie, burning everything, and everyone she came into contact with, and cared less. Then, at the end of that awful and dark time, when her own fires inside died and she was burned to her bones, she started back. She made herself a promise to reign over herself again and never let that happen again. Like her first walk out of the posh house in the hills she was first interned in, she claimed that same resolve, that strength and desire never to let it happen again.

She decided to have her baby now, and never look back. And at the end of her time in recovering, she and Art conceived Alex, naming him after the conqueror for her own memory of how she had deceived and hurt any and all she loved. Alex helped her conquer all. These things she withheld as inventoried and locked up evidence only held before herself, and not to him. Every day she stood straight in that fire of her memory, and burned like wax for her crimes against Art and her love for him. That, she told herself, was enough hairshirts to last a few lives.

Chapter Thirty

The conversation turned to the reunion in Los Angeles, and having both committed to attending there was an intrusion of anxiety into each crafted message. Tom started looking at himself in the mirror, his shock of hair, cut into a shorter version of when he was younger, and his face somewhat fuller, but still angular, and he wanted Nina to see him like before.

Mary, when they dressed for an occasion or some dinner somewhere associated with work, took inventory of him and thought to herself, *He still looks hot when he cleans up.* She always thought him attractive, and even now, knew it mattered to him to stay that way for her. They shared a truce in how they respected each other's space and hobbies. His was the world in the garage or his little office over the driveway, and she on her laptop in bed, her chocoholism evident on the nightstand. She'd get out of bed on occasion to take a break and peeked in on him, and at times find him in a dream state. She wondered where and who he was with. Once she startled him and asked where he was, that he looked like he was in a trance.

He felt a rush of instant guilt. He wasn't thinking of her, but Nina. Reliving a time when they talked about their own kids and the future. He wondered how we choose the roads we do, when Mary's voice held him accountable. How do you answer that he wondered, "Oh, honey, was just reminiscing about the old girlfriend and what our life together could have been." Not hardly. Not even close after being with someone two thirds of your entire fucking life and having a grown son. You don't go there.

It was a few days off from travelling to LA and Mary and he had a dinner engagement to attend in DC for a friend who was going to work in the Department of Education. They dressed quietly, jazz in the background on the iPod dingus that played the music through speakers. John Klemmer's sax weaving in and out of them as they looked for socks, hose, ties, slips. His shirt out of his pants as he pulled up his collar to run his tie around his neck and pull the ends down, concentrating on measuring the ends for the right hang when done with the knot.

Mary had stopped pulling her hose up a long brown leg to watch him. She caught the look on his face as he threw one end over the other, his hair polished and smooth from his recent shower, but knowing soon it'd dry into sharp edges from his duck tailed brushing and falling out of its coiled roll in front, like the perfect tube in a wave feeling the shore, falling into itself. His hair would follow suit, and later over drinks, he'd look almost boyish with the exception of the bone white hue of age he carried. In that second, taking that mental picture of him, she wondered what life without him would be like. She shivered at the coldness it brought.

She started to open her mouth to ask him why he hadn't

confided in her, cried to her, screamed in anger as to what fate had decided for him, but held the words back. Klemmer whispered "...*Touch*..." and she threw her head back, keeping a tear from dropping down her cheek. Mary never wore makeup so he wouldn't see any telltale tracks of mascara. She turned away, glancing at him as he pulled the bottom of his tie down and straightened the knot. Was he sparing her? Was he afraid of hurting her? Scaring her?

They lived in and out of each other so much, doing things for the other without speaking or making a gesture, just anticipating, knowing, and yet ... he was dying or on the verge of dying and he tied his tie, looking her way, curling the side of his mouth in that Tom smirk she knew to mean, "Hey, aren't I an asshole?"

"Fucker!" she wanted to scream.

Sometimes she'd slide back into island pidgin in certain instances, her secretary asking her what she said not comprehending...she remembered *bumbye*...island speak for "by and by...bygones"...things will work out...she said to him, "Bumbye, kan'e."

She had found his stash of papers, knowing all his hiding places as well as she knew the back of his neck in a crowd. She saw his lab results accompanied by the doctor's personal letter. She would allow him some latitude; give some advantage to him on this. After her anger and fear she had to be island, she had to give time for him to heal inside...to tell her. That was the way, so she took it inside and kept her peace, the pain at times unbearable and released like steam from an overheated radiator, hot and smarting, the pressure drop only momentarily alleviating. *Fucking men*, was her departing thought every time, since reading his medical paperwork.

Tom pulled his jacket on, a dark navy suit, Cremiuex soft white shirt with a dark blue silk tie, his hair out of reflex already boyishly unruly as it dried, looked at her.

"How do I look, honey?"

Mary gave an upper lip eating the lower sort of holding back a laugh or tears type of smile.

"You look fine, haole-boy…"

Chapter Thirty-One

He had an afternoon flight that got him into Los Angeles, with the time change, at around four P.M. He was seated and having a drink, also mellowed by a mild analgesic controlling his cough. He had an argument with the oncologist about starting and getting his act under control, but Tom wasn't sure yet. He hadn't talked to Mary either, and still didn't have an answer as to his hesitancy. It was the first time in his life he was faced by his maker, and he was almost rolling it around in his mouth, as if he tasted some new wine on the fly at Trader Joe's. He just couldn't find his voice either, wondering if he were frozen in the road, headlights almost on him transfixed like certain road kill. He wanted to read, but he couldn't, so he just sat and thought about things. He thought of his morning and how he and Mary showered together. When they first started living together, showers were a ritual. They had to be together, washing each other, kissing, soaping up, Mary lifting a leg, and staying locked together until the water was cold. Then after the birth of their son, the showers sort of drifted apart, another maritime ritual given up. It was sporadic and they both wondered, separately, why they didn't do it more often. Tom walked into the bathroom after the alarms had been snoozed and milked to death and Mary already inside to shower and bolt for work, so he watched her through the opaque glass, her blur of hair visible and her brown skin, searching for what her hands were doing. He watched her as she washed or rinsed her hair, chimera-like in the rolling of the glass, as if she were something submerged, seen under the ice in a slow current. He watched her silently as though he were in a peep show, holding his breath lest someone in the booth next to him heard or mocked him.

But this morning, she made it a point that they intersected at the shower, and that he accompany her inside, called him in. Once there, she started soaping him with the body wash, smiling, like she would when they were in their let's-fuck-and-drink-Coronas-all-night-binges. Her hair was partly wet so in places it was dry and others it was heavy and hanging with water, curling down like some blackened vine. He looked at her hard, small nipples; chocolate kisses. Like that day in Kapiolani Park hardened from the surf and material of her black bikini top making him follow her, thankful his eyes were parked behind shades.

"Here haole-boy…soap me up," she said, after handing him the body wash bottle.

He filled both hands with the gel and started massaging it into her shoulders, working down. She watched him rub her skin, thinking of the thousands of times he'd done this, enjoying each one, knowing he'd touch her the way she liked. She'd never been bashful when they were alone, and told him what she liked and wanted. He did as she asked always, only smiling, never saying a word. He knew what she liked to play in the shower, and he started running his fingers, soapy and smooth, between her lips. She turned a leg out so he could fill her slit with his fingers, her hands on his shoulders for balance, just like she did now. His fingers wet and jellied slid over her clit and her hole easily and she dug her fingers into his shoulders.

Her voice lowered and urgent, telling him he was doing it just that way he did and she pushed his fingers down inside her as she started rubbing her own clit. She was wet inside, and he knew if his fingers were inside her and she was touching herself, she'd come quickly.

She panted on him as he slid another finger inside her, the thickness of them together making her start pushing her hips forward and back. Her voice always took on another sound altogether when she ran up the steps to orgasm, wild and out of breath, until she announced she was, and there it was, her free hand grabbing his hair hard, pulling it, his head closer to her, her mouth ready to kiss him as she came on his fingers, legs heaving about, then started giggling and pulling his hand away, her signal for all clear.

He thought about that as he sat in his seat, 40,000 feet over New Mexico, his fingers under his nose, reflexive. He couldn't smell her trace anymore, but knew it and could without it present. He decided to nap and let his memory fade away, his vision of Mary like smoke, dissipating and shape changing as he settled down into this chair and closed his eyes. He was erect just thinking of her.

He slipped back into his thoughts of being in between the two women; riding up and down the waves as he floated, rising and falling.

Polonio Pass

Remembering so many things Nina had said and pieces and songs she played for him when they hung out, sometimes cutting classes to be together. Then the times he and Mary took what they called 'mental hygiene' days, a joke among educators in maintaining sanity. They made sure Mary's folks knew they weren't working that day when Drew was in school, and they drove out North Shore and surfed Haleiwa or maybe Waimea if it wasn't huge. When they moved off island to the mainland, they explored the countryside or snuck to DC and spent a day on the mall, weaving in and out of the museums.

How would that have gone with Nina? They traveled to Palm Springs, San Diego, and San Francisco together never having ever crossed a state line. Mary and he had been to Europe, Japan, Oceania, and many of the lower forty-eight. So many different places it made him and Nina's small sorties look juvenile. In the thirty plus years it all seemed juvenile. Back then he hadn't a clue as to what he was doing in life, just carelessly pinballing in between women, some he couldn't even remember their faces or names. His drinking with the shipyard guys and running his bike at the redline, buzzed insanely and hoping Celeste and her big round ass were home and waiting. He was then out of control and looking back; amazed that he didn't kill himself. Kill himself. Was he killing himself now as he flew west?

Tom slipped in and out of his life as he replayed one time against the next as if he were editing film drunkenly, randomly throwing images up on a screening room wall. He looked at pictures of the Polonio Pass online, the road bracketed on each side by the brown rolling hills of a middle California landscape, the light from the west telling it was afternoon as Dean had headed west on this same highway into the new autumn sun. In one picture it was as if the photo were shot in sequence of Dean's ride, late afternoon looking down the pass as he and his mechanic in the silvery Spyder slid into the valley.

He imagined the gear changes and the sound it must have made, then thinking of his Triumph pipes, and how when he opened the throttle they'd reverberate like fat hollow drums. He liked how when he did that to Nina or Mary or the few others he'd thrown on the back had reacted. Grabbing him and either looking over his shoulder to see the oncoming road or placing their heads down and becoming a part of him. In that instant, he felt guilty that he'd let the repair of the Trident in his garage go on so long. What was he waiting for? *Not getting any younger*, ran laughing through him. It felt like a goose walked over his grave. A cold shiver. He looked out the window of the plane, the deserts below with their dull and cloud punctuated relief yawning back at him.

What would LA be like?

Chapter Thirty-Two

She looked at Art from behind as he read a magazine and she smoked outside, a hot day for April. She wondered how many people actually studied their mate's heads in absolute detail. She always enjoyed examining him when he wasn't aware of it. As if she were hiding in the bush, invisible with her stripes in the high grass, observing him as prey, watching and studying his actions. She was doing some work on an awful script a friend had dropped off, having given up themselves and needed her expertise in exhuming it, re-examining the corpse of the work, and making it alive again. She took a drag, tossed the bound work onto a glass outdoor table and knew it was DOA and no one could salvage it.

"Utter shit," she said to herself. She went back to spying on her spouse.

Art had again asked about the reunion, and again, she answered in the affirmative. He'd been studying *her* then. In the past, he felt different things about Tom, knowing his history with Nina quite well. They included respect, hatred, and a shared understanding of what they had attempted to saddle at one time, probably being thrown the same distance. When Tom was first revealed to him, he was jealous. He wanted to have known Nina then, when her body was untouched, her gray eyes not so full of irony, wore a ponytail, and rode a motorcycle. He punished Tom in his mind, feeling that he embodied the old saw, 'youth is wasted on youth' and didn't know the treasure he had in his hand. He held that younger image of Nina, captured only in photos now, on a pedestal. Then at other times, he didn't hate Tom so much as wishing to actually talk to him and pump him for an unexpurgated history of Nina.

Kelleher filling in the blanks, many of which were erased by either drink or pill. In the beginning he felt as if he were obtaining a travel booklet brush stroke of her existence, much of which she either didn't remember or failed to transmit. He hated hearing Tom's name erupt in so many conversations at her parents' house as well, it seeming he was practically a family member for years. Art reflected on these feelings and then felt disgusted that he'd been angered over the memory or mention of a boy from years ago, who may not even be alive anymore. Feeling that way when she wore *his* wedding ring, shared *his* life.

The worst time had been when she had lost the baby, and it took every bit of him down to the bone to keep her from hurting herself, him, and others. It was touch and go in one or two places and once during a heated moment, when she was hospitalized and not back at the silliness of the plush rehab institute, she invoked Tom to help her. Save her. That stung. Coming out of nowhere during a free for all, and Nina pulling a *Lost Weekend* scene. Later, over coffee in the cafeteria of the hospital, he tried let it go, knowing it was random, but still it hurt to hear it. He found her stash of pictures, boxed up and pushed under magazines and old *Rolling Stone* editions from the late 60's to the mid 70's. There were cards from holidays, birthdays, and a cut out of Mr. Goody-Good from *Winchell-Mahoney Time* that was just insanely crazy, shaking his head at her collection of treasure; a bunch of Polaroid's, old 35mm's, and some 5x7s and 8x10s. He finally saw Tom, immediately hating him for his hair and then just as quickly laughing at that thought. There were pictures of him alone or with her, or just her, the bike and her and him on the bike. One picture was of him, in what Art figured was his usual attire, jeans, faded tee, pocket with cigarettes, and high top sneakers. Art liked his smile and studied it. Seeing what Nina saw. A good-looking lad. And if he walked up to Art, he'd break Tom's fucking neck.

Nina put her cigarette down and ran both hands through her hair from bow to stern. Corinne was coming over to show her what she was wearing to the reunion, which was tomorrow night, and she wondered if she had made a mistake. She and Tom started down a path she wished to avoid, and yet here she was. It came up in their messages, and that was how she still affected him, now that they had reconnected.

Nina felt it too, yet had not wished to cry havoc and let slip that fact. But she did. She'd been fucking Art a lot the last week. Ambushing him out of nowhere, even topping him and telling him in details what he had to do to her. Fires lit from long ago.

He would watch her sleep afterwards, wondering about her, always a mystery to him in some way. Only he and Kelleher really loved her. That silly man she married before had no clue about her. That's what rubbed him about Tom, because he had truly loved Nina. He wasn't some dipshit fly by night. He had been firmly in her life and had probably done before what Art did now, listening to her breath moving against the sheets, her hair thick and tied loosely. He grudgingly gave Tom his due, but humorously, still swore he'd snap his neck given the opportunity.

Chapter Thirty-Three

Tom thought of contacting his brother's widow, Marty, and then thought better of it. No use kicking *that* dead horse. He had no ties left in California at all. When he got his rental at LAX, he drove straight to the old neighborhood and couldn't recognize anything going, there, or coming back. The house he lived in when he and Nina started sparking wasn't even there anymore. A large; modern two story had grown over it using the one story ranch as a foothold. Only the one eucalyptus that bordered the neighbor's house was left.

"Wow." He sighed. "What a difference. Dad and P.J. would flip out seeing this." He was certain all of his old neighborhood and Los Angeles had undergone some serious renovation in architecture and demographics. He hadn't been back in so long he got lost finding his way to the hotel he was at, just up the street from the reunion, not wishing to stay in the same place it was housed.

It was late for him since he was on east coast time, and after driving through his old neighborhood, was in that early evening zone for drink. So after checking in and arranging his room, he wondered should he go to the hotel bar. He decided to call Mary before it got too late. He'd been away before on business trips to symposiums and conferences and hated sleeping apart from her. It struck him that they had barely been separated save for her trips out, the longest maybe a week, and his small overnighters. They were for the most part inseparable. He felt a deep stab of guilt looking at his laptop knowing full well there was probably a note from Nina on it. Alone and thinking of Mary and his life together, Nina's e-mail was like a small and dangerous firearm, loaded and unlocked in a drunk's room ready to be played with.

He called Mary.

He caught her coming back from her swim as she was pulling up in the driveway. He pictured it as if he were watching from his window, she framed as if performing in a movie. Talking to him as she grabbed her things out of the car, stretching into the backseat for something and cursing in pidgin, then relating things of her day to him, three thousand miles away, his fingers having been inside her, his lips on hers, just hours before and now almost disembodied back in California. He felt untethered, truly that man floating in between the two ships, the bottom far under him, as he heard her voice and knew it so well; its rhythm and tone. He felt as if his sea anchor of gold had no more weight in these waters in which he had entered, a place that he was weightless and wasn't grounded to her as he had been before. Mary, even connected to him by voice seemed to become a distant landfall, a silhouette dark and small on a horizon that was fast disappearing in the loss of sunlight.

"Eh? You there?" she asked his line quiet.

It shook him out of his trance, "Yes, honey girl...I am here, just out of it from the flight, sorry. How was your swim?"

She frowned, now already in the house, her cell embedded in her shoulder against her cheek as she placed things down and opened the refrigerator to grab a bottle of Corona. "Already told you, the heating system was down and the water made my nipples hard enough to cut glass."

She asked herself, *Is he getting that damn old or is he on meds I don't know about, since I have become a mushroom here, kept in the dark and fed shit?*

"Hey, call me tomorrow, okay? I just got here and making something to eat."

There was a silence, and then Tom broke it, "I love you, Mary."

She giggled around a carrot she grabbed, "I love me too...thanks for this morning, haole-boy."

He smiled weakly, "My pleasure." But his footing was untenable as he hung up, and again he felt that free-swinging motion of a groundless Los Angeles under him, the only familiar landmark in front of him, Nina.

Mary looked at his side of the bed, now three hours ahead of Tom and already in one of his old bike tees and panties, reading. They hadn't made their bed that morning and his side was thrown away from the pillow that held the impression of his head. She pictured his white hair, spread like a straw fan over the material, always a crazy rooster tail when he awoke. She had seen that hair go from indigo to flat iron and finally snow, where it seemed loud, indestructible in the past, now it was mellifluous and fragile. What pain was he in and why was he suffering through this in silence? She ran a hand on his pillow, taking away the imprint of his head as easily as a rising tide smoothens a beach. She washed her hand over the entire area of the sheet that was exposed, a flat, and undistinguishable area now.

Chapter Thirty-Four

When she listened to the opening guitar of *Gimme Shelter,* she erupted into goose bumps and even though she had heard it probably over a thousand times, it still had the effect of having cold water thrown on her. Nina felt her nipples tighten as she stood in her closet, looking at the dress she had picked out for tonight. It was a simple, black cocktail dress, sleeveless with a plunging V-neck, yet elegant. She tried it on, her white, yellow hair crowning it nicely. She had cut it to her shoulders with long bangs and her face framed. Her face and its entire story, deciding to wear her life for all, and fuck them if they couldn't take a joke.

And Tom would see her too, and for him, she needed to be just as she was. She went to the volume switch and turned the music higher. She felt like she'd been drinking when she listened to this music loud. The sheer force of their music made her feel high and compensated for whatever mediocrity she suffered during the day, as if showering after enduring the most oppressive heat. Standing in her heels and panties, her heavy breasts exposed, she grabbed the hanger rail above her in the expansive closet and swayed her back and hair to the rhythms, wishing Art would walk in and just fuck her.

Downstairs, Art read through the script Nina had been trying to resuscitate, and he was absorbed in it. It was a melodrama about expats living in Japan and a has-been writer who was trying to be reincarnated symbolically as he toiled in a Japanese school where all the other *gai-jins* were fucking the students to death. He could see it playing. Nina dismissed it as total hooey.

In her back and forth with Tom on e-mail, they dished up people they schooled with and left no meat on the bone. It would be interesting to see them up close and then look at each other and laugh. Corinne had known Tom in school as well, but Nina had left him out of the conversation when Corinne had pumped her for information about whether or not he would show. She had seen him on Face Book as well, when snooping, and knew he lived in the mid-Atlantic region. Corinne called her and asked Nina if she saw him, and Nina played it off as if she hadn't the time, *but you can tell me about it.*

Nina wondered how they could hang and also be a tripod with Corinne, Tom sharing Art's position, no love for Nina's friend. In high school he respected her as Nina's friend, probably the only girl she was close to being one of those girls who naturally gravitated towards men as friends, eschewing the open hostility and bared claws of her female peers. She and Tom decided to play the reunion as a surprise for both, and let others draw their own conclusions. They'd also be able to allow Corinne to extricate herself if she hooked up. *Just weaving that web, aren't we?* She thought, her downturned smile unseen in the closet.

The rest of Gimme *Shelter* trailed off and she felt nervous, excited, and absolutely aroused at thinking of Tom, so guiltily, she went downstairs to model her dress for Art and gain his approval. Corinne was driving there, with Nina driving back as the DD in the case of Corinne inhaling a few too many cocktails. Art had even offered to drop them and come pick them up, to which Nina placed a wet towel on, stating her dad had performed those duties and those days were done.

Tom ran a brush over his suit, deciding before leaving home to not wear a sports coat and slacks. Mary told him to go aloha, with khakis, and a Tory Richards island shirt with beautiful koi on it. He felt he needed a suit, wishing to appear opposite peoples' memories of him as a biker, intending to display his position in academics. After forty years, he wanted to make a statement, and as petty as it seemed for him, it was right. He had no really close friends from those days since he and Nina were inseparable, and outside of P.J. and his motor head pals, had no real contacts. He hadn't lettered in sports, didn't attend any clubs, never attended a football game, had only class pictures in the yearbook of him in the shop classes, and no random on campus pictures because he stayed virtually locked in with Nina and didn't attend any rallies either. In regards to peoples' memories, Tom was a bit of a cipher and was always remembered as the guy who dated Nina, no recall of anything he had done himself. A few remembered his bike parked at school and how he dressed, yet if asked for solid information, no one could really state anything in detail. There were a few girls in his class year and below who had crushes and were of the 'envy and wish to be Nina' club, but they tended to lean more towards the Nina envy than Tom crush zone.

Will was his closest friend, in the sense that they shared classes and had miraculously kept in contact over the years. He also was a confidant of Nina's, having known her since grade school. Never being a threat, Tom liked Will as he just seemed to always be upbeat and funny, doing various movie bits for laughs. He worked on Will's car, and they stole beers from his parents' garage and they listened to music together and smoked Winston's. He visited him and Mary in the islands and also been a guest back east where they lived now. He was still single, joking that he was married to his chocolate lab and would also be a good smoke screen at the reunion too if it was uncomfortable between he and Nina, even after so much correspondence.

Tom dressed and decided to hit his hotel bar before leaving for the reunion, being held at a new hotel in Santa Monica. He was staying at him and Nina's old deco hotel on Ocean, amazed at the renovations and clean slate for his memory, somehow wishing it were the same old Chandleresque dive it was before. Just staying there, felt like cheating on Mary already. His room looked out to sea and he had only to dim the lights to have Nina's memory there among the empty bottles and cigarettes, nude and looking out at Santa Monica Bay talking about film and books, music and people. He smiled at the memory and left for the bar.

Chapter Thirty-Five

In some of his e-mails to Nina, he tried, when feeling wistful, to convey exactly what an impact she had on his life, his intellect to be specific. The books she fed him in a sense, and the day trips, if even by bus when non-driving teens to the art museum at Hancock Park all had an effect on him. They hadn't left him omniscient the day after, or the year after, but down the road when he started to really mature and understand his life through Mary, it all took meaning. Of course, he understood the books and the effect on him when he read them, but the layers of the stories didn't really bloom inside him until much later. Like the effect of laying out in the sun and not realizing it until you enter a dark room and your skin is still warmed and you feel that dizzying rush from leaving it outside.

When Tom read *Tender is the Night,* he was put off by the feeling he was reading two different books in one, and yet years later, he understood that it was two very distinct and different times and that was how the Divers had become. They were one thing at one time, and quite another later on. Like with Nina in the period of years they were invisible to each other. They had changed and it happened silently, within each other. When he read Mishima, at her behest, it took him time to understand the subtlety of his images, and again years later, understand through his books the narcissism both he and Nina owned and shared and how ultimately they did for themselves instead of each other and how very different it was with Mary, where he shared and knew what she needed and tried hard to be there.

For Nina, he'd been there, but only in body, allowing her to exert a fine and yet silent hold upon him. When she no longer needed to have him in that position, he was jettisoned and adrift, and his solace in Celeste's round ass, the sexual pirouettes of the ballerina, and the earthy funk of Lauren's small smoke-filled flat filled with jazz, was mostly fuck and fodder to fill in the spaces.

When he related to her this profound power she had on him, she was surprised that he had articulated it and made her see it with more clarity than she had ever thought about it in the time they were together. She knew she had him enthralled and in flux always, but to have Tom explain just how and what effect it had was to her comforting and a surprise at the same time. It filled her with a sensation of accomplishment and well-being. Her affection for him, always somewhere in her heart, was rekindled and felt boundless in a way that she hadn't felt in years. She never had someone tell her of the effect of her life on his or hers in such a way. Yes, Art had always communicated to her the positive influence she had on him and how she had given Alex so much, but Tom was that beginning, her proving ground, and she believed always in the past that she had damaged him forever in some way. Careless and selfishly like a child leaving something of value outside and having it stolen or desecrated.

She had no way of knowing what she'd done in the long run. And then here he was an academic and a professor who taught Humanities of all things, and a department co-chair. He was married for thirty years and had a grown son and a wife who looked like a Gauguin painting come to life. He was still funny, had stayed a liberal and remembered almost *everything* and helped back-fill some things that she'd forgotten in her chemical or alcoholic periods. He was interested in her family and her marriage, asked many questions about her son and his studies, how he was almost graduated from college, and just little odd and ends about her and Art, and she was overjoyed she could tell him these things.

Tom and Nina had grown past so many things apart, and seemingly arrived at the same place, content, and comfortable in their skins. Yet under it, there was a small amount of heat that was unmistakable as fire. They both felt it and they talked around it, walking slowly and every so often so close to it, they felt it as if it were on their skin, in their clothes. As he sat in the bar waiting to go, he felt the old heat as if it were covering his dermis like a fine silk, clinging to him and while cool, kept the heat inside at a constant level. He agreed that it was not a heat he could drink away.

As she stood in her black dress looking out the window for Corinne's car, she wondered if she should have worn a pad in her underwear as that same film of warmth covered her and made her feel as if she were on a first date, anxious and excited.

Chapter Thirty-Six

He tried to find it as if it were a line of debarkation in his life, the period he started to really think of life and who he was. The times where he listened to music at home, Gene Pitney wailing about *Liberty Valance,* listening to untold Link Wray instrumentals and not being glued to the television for *Combat* every Monday. The line had been Nina and her society and cognizance. He smiled wondering how things might have been for him had he never known her and just settled for a Marty like his brother, content with someone who only knew she was there to open his beer and breed somehow with a bee-hive hair-do intact.

That very first time he had the nerve to visit Nina's house, taking the big blue bus there, and walking the three blocks from the stop. After he had sweat through his shirt after meeting her folks and getting asked at least forty-five questions it seemed. She gave him *Catcher in the Rye* and told him, "You remind me of Holden." He just smiled like a twit and took it and the kiss on his cheek. He felt it the entire night. When he left, he lied and said he was being picked up, not having the balls to ask his dad to get him and certainly not asking P.J. who would have walked to the door and embarrassed the shit out of him. Her dad, who still wore a tie at home, meeting P.J. who probably had his Pussy Galore's Flying Circus tee shirt on. So he walked home holding the book, stopping to read it under lampposts.

He arrived at the hotel where the reunion was being held, and seeing the signs for Revere High, followed them around a huge winding lobby of loud carpet and boutiques. There was a small bar of what looked like the Jetson's living room, with long oblong pendants over the small bar beckoning him that was the signature of the new boutique hotels. But he walked by and found the tables in front of the open ballroom doors, balloons and a blow up of the class picture and school. There were three women manning the table, with a few people milling about on the periphery, and some half drunken glasses on a table filled with place cards and name tags.

Tom straightened his tie and walked up smiling. "Hello…Tom Kelleher."

The woman he spoke to looked at him and then checked her list. Tom stared at her hard, wondering who she was, as he attempted to fit her face into a younger one in the manner they do on the forensic shows on A&E. He couldn't place her to save his life. She shuffled thru some stickers with peoples' names.

She smiled, "Here you are, Tom! Do you remember me, I'm Beth?" Tom finally glanced at her nametag, and then still not remembering, smiled broadly and said, "How have you been?"

Beth, all perky, which for fifty-seven or eight seemed a bit odd to Tom, smiled again and said, "I have been wonderful…wonderful husband and wonderful kids and life! How have you been, you silver fox you…look at all that white silvery hair! God, more than half the men here are bald or going there."

"I'm good…good. I'm married and have a son in grad school."

Beth had somehow managed with fluid movements to secure a place card and his nametag in a small little bundle with a program and handed it to him. Tom thanked her for it and as he walked away, had a quick flash in his head after seeing her smile, "You were a cheerleader right?"

Smiling, Beth jumped out of her seat and as if she had pompons, shouted "Revere is here!"

Tom smiling walked into the ballroom filled with about a hundred or so people, some sitting, men mostly standing in small groups talking. There was a sound system/DJ set up and *Let's Spend the Night Together* was playing. He recognized no one. He had to put his glasses on in the din of the room, lights turned down probably on purpose to give an assortment of middle aged people the benefit. He immediately turned in the direction of the bar and walked there casually, not wishing to give the impression he had just come from the bowery. The song ended and a guy's voice, loud and booming came over the room,

"Hey…the Stones…and sorry no Iron Butterfly until the drugs take effect! Remember this?" Immediately Country Joe and the Fish started, *Sweet Lorraine*. It was like jumping into a pool of 60's music, insane. He made it to the bar and ordered a Stoli rocks, wondering if he had been smart to do this. A man came up next to him to order. He was a few inches shorter than Tom and wore a very smart and tailored suit. His face was serene and although his hair was slipping back on his head, was thankfully making no maneuvers to comb it over or push it forward like Zero Mostel used to. Tom studied him as he dropped a tip into the jar and the man waited for his drink.

He turned to Tom. "I know you. You're Tom Kelleher. Didn't have to read your name. Your look…you still wear it in that longish DA you did in school, 'cept now it's all white. You dated Nina Hassel. Always thought you would get married, but saw her ten years ago at the 30th and she was stag, hanging with Corinne what's her face"

Tom was so surprised, he was speechless as he studied the man's face, thinking to himself that he really didn't spend a lot of time in school socializing and having male friends. He smiled a little bit and told the man, "No, we did not," and then reading the man's name tag without seeming too obvious, remembered him as a guy he had classes with throughout high school, barely talked to and also knew he lived in Nina's neck of the woods. At parties this guy was in the peripheral or with other guys of his cut of cloth.

"Hi Charlie…so how have you been?"

Charlie, had gone to work for his father in Los Angeles in a bottle printing business that had turned out quite well, took it over, moved to the Pacific Palisades, and then up north to Carpentaria where he had a huge ranch in the rolling hills. Occasionally he drove into LA and visited or had dinner with his wife and a few friends. He was planning a wedding for his youngest daughter.

Charlie smiled somewhat wistfully. "Is she coming…Nina?"

Tom straightened himself out and said, "I don't know, haven't checked the RSVP online. Wouldn't be surprised if she didn't live in Europe or someplace. Were you a secret admirer, Charlie?" Tom asked as if they were old conspirators, laughing at that thought.

"We were all hoping she'd dump you. In school," Charlie smiled, embarrassed a little at his impromptu confessional. "There were quite a few of us. We all wished we were the rear seat of your Triumph, if you get my drift"

Tom put his drink down, rubbed Charlie's head, picked it up again, and walking off said, "I hope it fueled your circle jerks," and strolled off. He muttered to himself, silently "Yes, Mary, I won't do it again."

The DJ was playing Cream now. Tom went to find his table after peeking at his place card and decided to get situated. He didn't want any more Charlie's popping up out of the woodworks, since it seemed his bike seat was a topic of conversation. His table was empty and just as well. He thought of Mary and wondered should he call her? It was already late in Maryland and he decided not to, they talked earlier and she seemed as if there were some questions she needed answered, but were just not asked. He could always tell when she was poking. But then broke off wishing him fun, don't hurt his back dancing, whatever dance haoles did to old rock 'n roll and kissed him over the phone.

Who would he dance with?

Nina saw Corinne pull up and walked into the living room where Art sat listening to an old Johnny Cash album. She laughed,

"Well, you can take the boy out of Kansas, but you can't take the Kansas out of the boy. Corinne's here." She leaned over and kissed his shaved head, the smell of his skin so familiar, so warm. "Good night."

Art turned down the music with the remote, "Remember, call me if you need a ride, okay? Don't rely on her if she's trashed or throwing a leg on someone." Nina smiled, donned her black shawl, and went out the door.

Corinne sat in her BMW knowing she had on too much make-up, but also knowing the lights would be forgiving. She watched Nina exit her house and walk towards her, the light from her porch behind her forming a halo around her silvery head. She was excited to be going and to see everyone. She was also excited to be Nina's 'wingman' and to be associated with her. Their friendship had gone all the way back to elementary school. She hoped she died first and Nina attended her service and thought good things about her. If Nina went first, she'd feel terribly alone. When she got into the car, Corinne smelled something familiar, but couldn't place her finger on it. "What is that you have on?"

"Shalimar. I used to wear it in the 60's, so apropos tonight." It was the perfume she wore the first time she and Tom had a date at the movies and madly made out for the entire double feature. She hadn't worn it in years and picked it up when shopping earlier in the week.

When she opened the bottle in the store, she thought she would fall over, the scent triggering so many different thoughts and emotions, as if she had fallen into a deep pool, surrounded by a warm sensation of a man. She felt his silken black hair sliding in between her fingers, almost impossible to hold, so she had to grab clumps and move him as they kissed in the balcony. They slowly dissolved into each other, over and through the arms of the movie chairs. He tasted only her lips, smelled only her perfume, and thought of nothing but the two of them alone in the entire theater. She shared his emotions as they kissed, his hands staying away from her breasts, satisfied to hold her, feeling her hair as it splayed over his hands as she held her shoulders.

Nina ran her hands under her hair, lifting, and spreading it out as she sat in Corinne's car. It fell over her shoulders and barely covered over her shawl. She thought of Tom in that dark theater and the smell of Art's head. She never understood how things like that collided.

They traded pleasantries with Beth, a woman who always made Nina's skin crawl when she approached her, asking for votes for whatever student office she coveted, and always asking Nina to come and try out for cheer. Corinne was almost ignored by Beth, who focused her attention on Nina and that also pissed Nina off.

"Well, welcome to you both…and Nina, I saw one of *your* old friends earlier," Beth said coyly.

Walking in, Nina turned to Corinne and said softly, "And who the fuck would she know who *my* friends were?" Making Corinne explode in a small, but sharp laugh.

She let her eyes get comfortable in the dark and stood there with Corinne, walking in to find their table. She saw a few people in groups, mostly men standing, and a few scattered tables where women sat talking, some with what looked like bored spouses sadly sitting and drinking.

She looked to the bar and saw a tall slender man with white hair in a Dean-doo walking away from a shorter man who was flipping off his back and knew instinctively that had to be Tom. She smiled, watching the man at the bar throw his drink down hard, and then ask for another. Instead of walking to Tom, she slid over to the bar. She came up on the man's right shoulder. She caught the bartender's eye.

"Ginger Ale, please" she said.

Charlie realized someone was next to him and turned as she ordered. He was breathless when he realized who she was, never forgetting her face in profile, full on, or in half shadows in yearbook pictures.

"What timing," he said slyly. "And here I was, led to believe you lived in Europe, maybe."

Nina looked at his name, recognized the older face from the younger version, and said, "Hello Charlie," smiling over her drink forgetting, he was at the last reunion. "So how have you been?"

"You look great, Nina. Beautiful. I enjoyed talking to you at the 30th."

"You talked to me? And why would you believe I lived in Europe? Whatever brought that rumor up?"

Charlie grabbed his tie with one hand and laughed, "I just saw Tom Kelleher, and he said you might live there, I don't know. I guess if anyone knows its him."

"No…I live here. I only fly to Europe when Tom Kelleher and I need to fuck our brains out. I thought that's why he rubbed your head." And she walked away, wondering if he was flipping her off, too. She walked straight to where Tom sat alone, at his table, nursing his drink. He looked good in his dark suit. She couldn't tell if it were a black, a deep charcoal, or navy in the poor lighting. His tie was thin and tightly knotted and his collar fit his neck. She had to laugh that it took another woman and thirty plus years to get his ass out of Levis and biker shirts. He sat there staring down at a small reunion program, not seeing her walk up, wanting to distance himself from Charlie and whoever else wanted to be the rear part of his banana seat on the Triumph, wondering how many touched it where it was parked during the day in junior and senior year.

She stood looking down on him. She went straight for *The Big Sleep*, "You're not very tall are you?"

Tom, the shock of her voice fixing him as if he were encased in cement up to his shoulders, still smiled, and spoke his line, "I uh, try to be."

She sat across from him and they just looked at each other. She found herself smiling and nodding her head as he looked, melting away her years, standing in another fire unlike her skin- rending bouts when she drank, but a warm flame that felt comfortable and healing.

Tom remembered Gatsby and Daisy, having taught that book in school and fell back on their moment when time stood still; his default. And he smelled the Shalimar and was thrown back in the theater, making out. Nina, no matter what was still Nina, even under the burden of years, and the changes on her that were obvious. They talked in letters and short messages since they had reconnected, and there she was, with her turned down smile and beautiful crown of hair. His first lover; her first lover. Corinne crashed the moment placing her drink on the table and sitting down behind it.

"This is labeled as the pregnant pause, I guess? I've been standing here for a minute as you two became statues." She looked at Tom, "Hello Tom…you look great! I didn't even know you'd be here."

Nina, recovering, "Or me either. A pleasant surprise! So where are you living, Tom, tell us all about it."

And so it went, small talk as they all played with their drinks, taking turns, then greeting others who sat down with their placards, and people remembered or didn't, and then Nina and Corinne got up to go to their respective seats since the place filled up and there were some announcements from the DJ/emcee. Tom felt as if the entire scene was dreamlike and if the people around him remembered or not, didn't mean anything. He loathed making small talk, but he did it automatically, thanking compliments he received for his staying fit or keeping his hair. He really didn't remember all the people at his table, two of which were letterman with their wives who vaguely remembered him for his bike, but knew who Nina was. He moved his chair so that he could see where Nina was, feeling that excitement when he saw her in the hallway passing, or sitting in class, leaning over to him, passing a note to him smiling before the bell rang. He watched her, sitting next to Corinne, smiling and laughing, turning to glance at him, catching him looking just as he would when he did in school.

He thought of Mary and he strangely felt guiltless. They didn't have this history, it was something stored in a book she wasn't a part of, not mentioned in any chapters. That time of his life hadn't commenced yet, and he realized he had to live through his life with Nina to make it to Mary and to stay there. This was something that was apart from her, and he tried to feel something that would impede him, make him dislocate himself, but he couldn't. He planned to be here, and now, settled in his chair, made his bed so to say and was comfortable. The conversation surrounding him was white noise, and he heard the music in the background as they sat drinking and conversing. He was content to send looks her way and feel fifteen again. There was nobody else in his life that occupied this special set of memories, the days when he needed to get away from his house and life and live in her world, her house even if momentary.

Corinne started questioning her the moment they left Tom's table, and all Nina could think of was how she felt seeing him, hearing Corinne, but not even caring what she asked. He looked at her as if she hadn't changed, that she was still that younger girl, the one she burned away and gutted, the one who lost her baby and destroyed people. That wasn't part of his memory of her. He saw the girl in the movie theater. She liked that, his seeing that Nina and loving her again. She needed to know that part of her lost past had a companion, and it was definitely requited. She saw him with his shock of white hair, and knew its texture, its feel. Her fingers' memory knew it too, having owned it so many times, captured it. She looked up and caught him smiling at her, and she smiled back in turn.

The emcee was bloviating about the yearbook sales in the lobby, and Paul Revere High gear. There were pictures being taken and jokes made about certain people who had shown up, class officers and BMOC's, cheerleaders and Beth leading a small cheer from the squad, those who could still muster one, and wasn't overweight or dead.

Tom started studying his old classmates and felt pretty good about himself. Many of the men looked like smaller eggs balanced on larger eggs, pates without hair, combed over, naturals that were once wild and Hendrix like were retreating to backs of heads or sporting the monk look of a bald skullcap. A few of the men cut a good figure still and it was obvious there had been some augmentation in breastland as well. Some of the women looked seriously moneyed and had athletic builds that he envisioned swinging a five iron at a country club. He caught a glimpse of Charlie sitting next to a woman who looked bored and with him the Shreft brothers, whom Tom shared a mutual disgust for. He caught one sitting on his bike and when confronting him, then realized he had been set up for a two on one. High school shit, boy-sauce levels too high. It had been a verbal standoff and some spit directed at his bike, but the ill feelings had lingered until graduation. Seeing them brought the disgust back as easily as his feelings for Nina. Is this what reunions were about besides just entering these emotional rooms and running the gamut from ecstasy to repulsion? Did anyone ever really leave high school?

"Hey!" Will slapped him on the shoulder, coming out of nowhere.

Tom smiled and stood up to greet him, "Right on time, Will…what's up? Good of you to make it."

"Shit, for what I had to fork out for this soiree, no way I'd miss it. But we should've just met at Barney's in Hollywood and drank there, the bill would've been the same and in much better surroundings and we could've gone jeans and commando." There was an empty seat at Tom's table so they maneuvered it around and Will parked next to him.

"Nina's here," he told him.

"Indeed? Well and how did that go…or haven't you talked yet?"

"Oh we just said hello's. She's with Corinne." He gave Will a lopsided smile. Will gave the same grin back.

"Does anyone remember you?" Will asked.

Tom thought on that, "Yes, if you asked someone, who was that bump attached to Nina Hassel or how many dreamed they were the seat of my bike," he said it matter-of-factly.

"Ohhhh…I see. Well, nice thing to be attached to," Will smiled.

Tom scrunched up his mouth before talking, "It's as if I wasn't even there, now that I think about it."

Will laughed, "It's high school, we all wish we weren't there! But, I'm going to stagger around and meet people I can't stand, and others that can't stand or remember me." And he went off. Tom looked up and saw Nina beckon him over. He rose and went.

A woman, next to her husband who had attended Revere, asked about Tom, and did he know him. "I think I do, but not sure."

"Striking hair," his wife said.

◎|◎|◎

Nina was involved in a conversation with a woman Tom recognized as Sheri, one of her friends from school who disappeared up to Berkeley after graduation. Sheri had that money look and was in great shape, her toned arms in a sleeveless dress. Her hair, gone to gray naturally was swept up to one side and her neck, while showing her age was still lithe and appealing. A man was standing over her in a very expensive suit with his hands in his pockets, in a pose he seemed comfortable in and used to. He took him to be her husband. Tom walked up and greeted her and Nina and Corinne.

Corinne of course chimed in first pretending as if they hadn't talked before, "Hello TOM...wondering when you would wander over, you look absolutely great, and kudos for not going all Grecian Formula on us."

Tom smiled graciously, "Thanks Corinne. You look well. Nina, Sheri...good to see you."

Sheri gave him a small and insignificant hug and turned him to the man behind her immediately, "Tom this is Rolf, my husband." Rolf extracted a hand from his packet and Tom felt its warmth, wondering if he had been hugging his balls with it. "Very glad to meet you," Rolf said, slightly accented.

"Likewise." He found himself staring at Nina and broke off, not wishing to be seen doing so, Corinne watching him now. Will came out of nowhere and started doing his Alex and his droogs routine, a high school favorite of his. Corinne laughed. Sheri was involved in politics up north after her time at Berkeley, where she took sociology and marched in protest against the war. Many class members had gone up north to school, in the bay area, Tom holding that against his blue collar Lake Merritt studio and Raiders games, not in school, but as a seaman. He gauged his inner feelings and felt nothing. He wasn't happy, sad, angry, or anxious. He was more bored than anything and wished to just sit and talk to Nina, ask her about her family, find out about the holes in their lives, and fill them in, and he hadn't noticed her table was becoming a nucleus of more people joining on the periphery, either stopping or seeing who was there. Even the DJ made a mention of it, and started playing *The In-Crowd*. Did he feel jealous? He did…there was a small feeling of it, like when in school and he couldn't gather her attention in abundance, and he was pissed off he felt that way. But what better place to feel it, he reckoned. Great to relive idiocy! The Stones' *Time is on My Side* came on, and out of the blue, Sheri stood up and grabbed Tom, brushing past her husband and asked if he wanted to dance. Surprised he took her hand and led her to the dance floor.

It was almost a surreal moment for Tom to even be holding Sheri's hand, let alone taking up her invitation to dance! The song, a semi slow blues lent itself to dancing together, so he took her in his arms. He could smell her richness; subtle and sensual and her body hard and fit under his hands. He found himself excited holding her.

"So Tom, what have you been doing these last 40 years?" And while a simple and appropriate question, from Sheri it was prying in its purest form.

"I teach at a small university in Montgomery County in Maryland. Humanities."

She held her head back to take him in and turned her mouth down in that 'wow, how surprising' attitude. "That's great...never would've expected it, honestly."

Smiling at her, "What would you expect, Sheri?"

Thinking a second, pursing her lips, "Thought for sure you and Nina would've married, divorced by now. You would've owned or worked at some auto or motorcycle repair place...have a huge beer belly." She laughed, "But not a teacher!"

"Stranger things have happened. Nina and I didn't make it past sophomore year in college, but you're right...I did fix bikes but only when I was putting myself thru UH."

Sheri pulled closer as they danced the middle of the song silently. Then looked up.

"You're married now?"

"Yes I am."

"But she's not here."

"No, she stayed home."

"Hmmm…" Laughing, she reached up and took the side of his head gingerly in her hand, and pulled his ear to her lips, " I had such a crush on you in school, but Nina would've murdered me, I am sure."

Tom was in shock. Sheri? Miss School Government, Social Conscience of the Class…him? "Honestly, I never knew." His surprise evident.

"This is the place we all confess isn't it, this small intensely weird bubble in time? Get it all off our chests? Too bad you were a remora to her shark"

The song ended, and again she stood on tiptoes and kissed his cheek, "Always wondered how nice it would've been to have sat on the Triumph. If you're ever in the Bay Area, call. " And she walked away as people applauded the end of the song, Tom standing alone and feeling like a jackass. Should, Woulda, Coulda.

◯◯◯

Earlier, after leaving his table, Nina started to feel the swarm of people around her and looked up to greet ex-girlfriends she couldn't remember being girlfriends with, and a plethora of husbands, men who admired her when younger and had slipped away from their wives, and of course, Corinne, as steadfast as a stone temple dog. Will slipped up behind her and tickled her, after his *Clockwork Orange* gig. She looked up, but there was no Tom, and knew he hated being in a gaggle, so would have to get his attention. He was sitting, surrounded by people, but he always seemed by himself even when in a crush of bodies. How curious he became a teacher, could stand in front of people.

She wondered how she'd fare teaching and felt nausea just entertaining the thought. She liked being in her den, her bed, reading, and editing alone. It's as if we're back in school, she thought, how weird. The lunch court, people moving around, the boom boxes that kids brought in with different music in every quad of the school...the DJ playing Marvin Gaye now, some people dancing. She wanted to ask him if he missed his Mary, wished he had brought her, and then knew what a dumb thing that'd be to say. He flew 3,000 miles without her. And there was just them. She finally got his attention and he came over and made small talk around the periphery of the table, with Sheri, who she couldn't stand in school, and a few other unfamiliar faces. As he talked, she watched him, his face, becoming more accustomed to who he was now, holding it against the Tom from her past. He had aged gracefully, a man who had few problems or if he did, handled them well. He kept his hair, and in a room of men who had lost that skirmish as sure as Pickett had lost his charge, had to accrue some envy or resentment from the men. Corinne had remarked to the same affect.

Just as Tom hadn't really thought that much of his image in high school, nor had Nina. She was as much an appendage on Tom as he had been for her, tunnel vision in their own little relationships and not having a peripheral life that included clubs, or close extended friends. They had, as her mother had told and warned, insulated her from other things and needed to break away.

What did he think of her now, seeing her after so long? Seeing her as she looked, after her battles? Art looked at her as a painting, a classic that had survived the years and occupation in other places to be admired. She wanted Tom to see her, as a woman he'd still fuck, not admire. And she was honest about it. She wanted to get out of her seat, leave the table, go talk to him, and grab him, wishing he had his bike outside. Be in high school one night, like Cinderella at the ball, and hop on the seat and drive off in that loud thumping of the pipes.

She leaned over to Corinne. "This fucking place is driving me mad! If Art was here he would've committed suicide already," she yelled over the din.

Corinne sipping a drink shook her head, hearing half of it. They both watched Tom dancing with Sheri, thinking totally opposite endings. Nina, to her chagrin felt jealousy. *How can I be jealous?* she wondered.

The DJ had started playing the Airplane's '*Today*' and the words seem to find their way into his past, stoking those fires harder…her own feelings starting to meet a head, the lyrics of the song placing her in 1967. It brought everything inside her to a head.

Nina found Tom's eyes again and stood up, pushing her chair into one of the Shreft brothers who was trying to see down her top. "See everything, Marshall?" Nina smiled. Marshall Shreft spilled his drink. Again she looked for him and caught his look, and she lifted her head slightly and towards the door.

Tom took this cue and left the table ahead of her, acting off instinct. He headed to the lobby, not even noticing how full the room had become. Corinne looked over at Nina, and seeing her rise, thought she was headed to the ladies' room so started up, but Nina's hand found her shoulder, and pushed her down. She got up, pulling her shawl off the back of the chair as she left. It resembled a windblown tree, branches pulling away from the trunk.

He stood in the lobby, the air cooler and not as supercharged with people, or so enclosed. He felt the sweat he hadn't noticed before, drying on his forehead and running his hand thru his hair, discovered it was faintly wet on his scalp. He saw Nina alight through the doors near the ones he had exited, and he turned and went out the door offered by the tuxedoed parking valet who asked for his ticket. But Tom looked for a cab, saw one and raised his arm. As he moved towards the cab, Nina swept into the open door ahead of him, the driver holding the door shrugging his shoulders at Tom, who just went past him and into the back seat next to her.

There was a moment that hung in the balance, like the last breath a hunter exhaled slowly before pulling a trigger. He barely got the name of the hotel off his lips before they were kissing.

Chapter Thirty-Seven

She hadn't tasted vodka in many years and Tom's mouth was like an explosion when they kissed in the cab. She looked at the room service menu, sitting as she had so many times in the past looking out to sea, her leg up relaxing nude. She smoked as she weighed whether to get a drink or not; she was sitting on a precipice and didn't at that moment care. In one night she had become an adulteress, left a friend alone without a word (and probably had Corinne spinning like a top) as she lounged nude; so ordering a drink didn't seem like a stretch, especially since she could taste Tom and vodka in her mouth.

The clear spring night allowed her to see out to the blackness, spotted here and there by a small vessel's lights beyond the breakwater. She let herself drift back to remember when they would spend a night, bottles and roach butts covering the room. Back then, there was no place to sync your iPod and listen to what you wished to, just a small clock radio with KPPC, KMET or KFWB; Sunday morning early a.m. hours on FM were Native American chants and strung out jazz. They listened to them all. She smiled to herself about those days and then decided she didn't need a drink after all, momentary folly, nothing more. Tom had his iPod and she could hear his collection of Stones and other retreads from bygone eras. Nina was impressed he liked Sublime though, and looking out to the darkness of the ocean on her coast, she wondered what his view of the Atlantic was like. She also didn't know what to do.

It was 1 A.M. when she had texted Art to explain that Corinne had drank too much, had driven her home, and was hanging with her, letting him know she was okay. She thought of the chickenshit method of texting and leaving it at that, but even the thought of doing that made her guilt want to drink a Stoli neat. Tom was quiet in the bed, almost on the verge of sleep and she thought perhaps she should plan a getaway and figure her excuse enroute to her house. She read all the messages that had piled up on her phone since midnight, and Corinne had pretty much guessed it, trying her best to couch it in a PC sort of way in case Art had looked at her phone, and was resigned to be Nina's beard for the night. Maybe that drink wasn't such a bad idea after all. Chickenshit.

Tom rolled over and was watching her, sitting at the window, holding that image against the ones from the past. Seeing the two women there simultaneously gave him comfort in a way. He felt warm inside having lived to tell himself he had seen both of them, and wondered how many people had reunited the beginning of their lives to the ends or near ends? There was poetry there somewhere, but in his state of fatigue, being three hours ahead and barely having slept, he couldn't find the handle. He sat up, running a hand through his hair and called her.

"Hey…" She heard him and turned and smiled a tired and

sorry smile. "We haven't seen each other in almost 40 years and then we go and step in it with our eyes wide open."

He pursed his lips and shook his head in the affirmative. "Yup…we certainly did. Do you need to go…make a call…what?" Tom was covered by the time difference, as it was only four in Maryland, and she wouldn't expect him awake until later, having tried to cope with jet lag and whatever. This was some sort of whatever.

She just smiled. She looked beautiful and tired, and had a sad peaceful look, he felt. There was a glass next to the bed that the ice hadn't melted in yet and he badly needed to drink something. Or hold his head under a showerhead. They had napped and then woke, smiling somewhat ruefully at each other.

"Want to shower?" He asked.

Nina felt that might be a good thing to do, so she acquiesced. Shower and get her head together, figure things out, make a move. *Jane says…*

Tom didn't know when it entered his head, but once it came in it, didn't go away. It was part way through the shower or before they had sex again. Cholame…drive to Cholame. Leave now. Drive all night and eat breakfast there. Just do it, never will if you don't go now. When he was seated at the reunion, he felt incredibly insignificant and invisible. He had lived his life, was a host now for a cancer and would probably slip away under the waves of life undetected. Yes, Mary and Drew would miss him, but what had he done? He scoffed at those thoughts and berated himself. He returned to the lecture of immortality he had with the students and couldn't think of anything he had done to make his memory a lasting one. It was only too obvious, just this night, that he had lived in Nina's shadow, basked in her sunlight, the nucleus from which he derived pleasure and sustenance either intellectually or physically. He was never a spiritual person and wondered if perhaps he should cover those bases now as he sat still undecided about starting radiation and chemo. Cholame...where Dean had in the twilight of that September day travelling at his speed become invisible to the kid in the station wagon who killed him. Could he do the same? Silly thoughts for a silly man, he laughed inside.

He turned his thoughts to Nina and when they had entered the room and started undressing. They both explored each other's old age as they peeled away clothes and ran hands over their bodies. Their last memories of each other was a dreamy glow of hard bodies and insatiable needs; now they both needed to lay down and not entertain any ideas of acrobatics or standing on one leg like a flamingo. They moved with stealth, but also moved slowly, making those last memories unable to stand against time, replaced by the present as it took their place. They could in no way fool each other or pretend that 'time had stood still' and would have felt obscenely embarrassed if one had uttered words to that effect. Nina, while still svelte, had lost her taught skin to time.

No quicker than pulling her hair to the side and kissing her neck did he discover her beauty failing. In that instant, Tom felt not only guilt, but also sadness and his own mortality magnified. He had pulled her on top of him, one of his favorite positions for making love to her, and took her in from the glow of the low lights in the suite. She had always had large breasts for her physique and they were heavier now, and still exciting to see. She sensed his enjoyment and sat up on him, leaning back and placing her hands on his thighs, watching his face. She tried to remember how he felt inside her when they played so much, and really couldn't find any memory, like an old ticket or keepsake left in a book as a marker. Tom wasn't that succinct a memory in that sense, yet when picturing them together making love it aroused her, just them together. She herself held him now against his image from years ago. A lynch pin of her memory was the night in Trancas when they were ill fated to rekindle their love after that tryst. He didn't look so dangerous now, and didn't move in the same violent way when he was near the end. It was almost as if he were metering their lovemaking, making use of every move, attempting to stretch every fiber he had to make it work and give her pleasure. He had, and she knew most of it was from history that finally exploded in this physical rendezvous; built up over the conversations in FB and emails; exchanged pictures and subtle innuendos.

Pictures rolled in Tom's head as he thought of them so long ago, and now making this reconnection back at a scene of the crime from their past was exciting him more. He had held her hips and then her breasts as they swung, Nina riding him faster now. He didn't need any pills now, he thought quickly, moving to orgasm with her, and how weird was that?

Chapter Thirty-Eight

The next couple of hours found them in and out of sleep, wrapped up on each other, then needing space, pulling apart. They could've been married for forty years in how they shared their bed. Tom sat up abruptly and felt it like electricity running thru him. Cholame. He would just dress and go, let Nina wake up on her own and call Corinne or a cab, but however she managed her escape, he needed to drive. He got up and started putting on his suit, pulling it off the chair and tree where his shirt and tie hung like loose flags on a windless field. He had other clothes unpacked but grabbed what he could and in his haste woke Nina, who pulled her hair to one side and focusing asked what the fuck he was doing?

"Cholame. I'm going…now. Don't ask, but I need to see it. Before I die."

She laughed, "Haven't we fucked up enough for one night? Now you want to drive some 200 miles or something and for what? Some teenage dream? A bucket list? Come on, Tom."

"It's in me…seeing you, being with you, I have to go." He pulled on his socks. "You weren't supposed to wake up."

"You're making enough noise to wake the damn dead." She

watched, curiously, enjoying the show by the elder Mr. Tom Kelleher, stuffing his tie into his coat pocket. "What do you need a tie for?"

He stopped and pulled it out of his pocket, curling his mouth at how many times he had done that coming home with Mary after a night out, just rolling it and stashing it away as he opened his shirt collar, relaxing.

"Habit," he said shrugging and then smiled.

She saw him, his face from so long ago inside this older, not unattractive man. "What do you think about my tits, Tom?"

That caught him and he had to pause. "I still like them. They're bigger now and heavier…and there's a certain eroticism to how they hang now."

She laughed, "That's about the best pc answer I've heard when it concerns old sagging tits! Thank you…I won't pass up a compliment! Now what in hell got up your ass to go there?"

He couldn't describe it and it had been brewing in him some time. It just was something he had to see, feel, take with him before he flew home, back to what he had to do, or not do. He felt light and full of energy. He felt invisible in the hotel ballroom, a mere shadow on a wall that a lamppost had left that passersby take no notice of. The light above him, looking up was Nina. Always Nina. He got it now.

He looked at her and slipping his feet into his loafers, reached into the mini bar and pulled out a couple of beers, candy bars, and a bottle of water. He smiled at her and gave that Gary Cooper two-finger roll salute that he had when they were pretending to be Tom Brown and Amy Jolly. And he walked out of the door.

Nina, sitting up nude, grabbed her dress and lingerie, started dressing quickly, also rifling through the mini bar.

Chapter Thirty-Nine

She woke up to a black interior, the unmistakable sound of wheels on the road, and in the middle of *No Expectations* and the beautiful slide guitar, Jagger's voice riding the tops of the guitar's notes. Tom had a rent-a-car he could use his iPod in, listening to his favorite music. She looked to the window and caught mostly her reflection in distortion and the inner lights of the dashboard. She looked at Tom, his face a calico of the dashboard lights. Her hand found his right arm, laying on the console between the seats and wondered why after so long even just touching him caused that familiar electricity. She saw him smile at feeling her touch and she asked if he could punch in the lighter, which he did, saying nothing.

"When did your hair go white?" she asked.

He laughed, "In my forties it started turning. Remember those pictures of my grandfather my dad had in the living room?   I guess he went white pretty young. What do you think? Make me look like an old geezer?"

"No…I like it. Does your wife like it, or ask you to dye it, or add that splash of gray like on TV?"

"She likes it. It just surprised her how bleached out it got so fast. Wasn't like I wasn't Casper the Ghost before," he laughed. "What color is your husband's hair?"

"Art's bald. He had the wrap-around thing going on and instead of how he says, looking like Fred Mertz, he'd rather go for the "Magnificent 7" look."

"Good call. I would probably like him, eh?"

Nina lit her cigarette and cracked the window to allow the smoke to escape, and it created a high-pitched wind noise in the car, making the music seem unbalanced and off key. Her left hand caressed his arm, almost in the fashion it would back when he drove her car when they went out. Strange, she thought, how easy it was to remember how she used to touch him and how reflexive it was. It was as if there had been no time in between the last time she did this. She reflected on their lovemaking in the hotel. She'd been almost hesitant to undress, hoping that he wouldn't find her unattractive, or worse, find her that way, and not being able to hide it, give himself away with a facial gesture. He hadn't, and in that she felt even more sexual.

She knew what had changed, and if he accepted it, then she had better just clam up and like that. She knew her skin lacked that suppleness from then and felt at times coarse and ragged. Drugs and alcohol had that habit of turning one into a shark. She'd also taken note of Tom; the once lean and hard ripped body had expanded, and while his height helped him appear slender, he'd gone soft in places she remembered that felt as hard as the chrome on his bike. But he still, at almost sixty, cut a good figure in his suit, and even as he stripped off, excited her, not being paunchy and his erection well defined. His hair almost bone white and that cock she rode so many times made her feel…wanton and crazy, once upstairs and able to fully be nude.

They had slowed down from their antics in the cab and once in bed, took the tempo of their sexuality easier, protracted. She knew she was contrary to his wife and made him leave the light on so he could see her and know that, I'm Nina…I'm not her…fuck *me.*

As she smoked and remembered, it also made her wonder guiltily how easy it had been to cheat on Art with Tom. She had thought of it many times and dismissed it out of hand, thinking she could never do that no matter…and what had it been? Minutes? No, not minutes, their e-mails and communications had been a prolonged foreplay; innuendoes, rekindled memories, and hints. She dropped her hand into his lap and again found him erect and smiled to herself.

Tom, feeling her hand there, blinked slowly like an owl, savoring her touch. His thoughts overlapped hers in questioning himself how quick he had given in and how he hadn't cared. Just leaving the reunion was liberating. He cast an eye on their correspondence and his trip planning and knew when he booked the hotel what he wanted. His memory of her sitting there nude discussing literature with him after drinking or smoking something, pizza boxes or empty cartons from the Chinese place down the street strewn over the tables and desks always gave him a mental rush. It was a month long seduction for both of them, and this was the end result, and streaking north of the San Fernando Valley also seemed normal at this time of the morning. Is it with some people that the string is never cut and just takes up where you left off? They were still over two hours away from Cholame. What filled Dean's head those last two hours?

His mechanic certainly wasn't feeling him up.

Chapter Forty

"I have to confess, I used to spy on you sometimes when you worked at that gallery in Santa Monica," he said.

She laughed, "For real? I'm flattered! I thought for sure you had cut the rope as I had so inelegantly done myself. I worked for a distant family friend, Averill. My mom helped set me up in that job and had no clue he and I were sleeping together or that he was bi. Yes…he was before you ask questions. I knew it, but didn't want to know it, right? So what would you do…? Use binoculars and stalk me?"

"Noooo…I used to be at that coffee house that sat kitty-corner to the entrance and stash my bike on the block behind it. I could see an angle of the gallery through the glass in front and at times see you walk to and fro."

"That pretentious faux Parisian place…in the rooms the women come and go/speaking of Michelangelo… I had to laugh sometimes at the phony-hooey I'd hear in there and have to go with. People who buy art just have money they don't know what to do with. He used to school me on answers about stuff that didn't show I was an ignoramus or smarter than the clients. Most of the stuff he showed was pretty much schlock"

"Somehow I can't see you as stupider than them. Remember when we horned in on people's conversations at the art museum…and talk all sophisto? That used to kill me. You had those tight black pants, your glasses and hair in a ponytail and look like you just swept in from Paris to chew over some art."

"We were always doing that…you would put me up to it." There was a pause. "Why did you spy on me, Tom?"

He winced in the dash lights, "I did it because I was jealous, still in love with you."

"But I know you were also seeing other women."

"They were fillings. Like for cavities. Like I have been a filling for people, too. Wasn't the same. I did a lot of that, I can say now, but it still didn't change inside what I felt. Make sense?"

"Yes, it does. When we were separated, I felt the same…first huge speed bump I hit with Averill, and I called you. Listen, you were the beginning of so much in my life, sexually and loving, there wasn't a template for me to follow, and you know what cold fish my parents are. Everything we did, the good things and mistakes weren't planned, and we invented them as we went along. We held each other aloft…and you probably don't know how much you kept me aloft, I guess I never really told you, but you did. I know you feel it was one-sided in that regard, but it wasn't. We didn't exactly communicate when it meant really spilling the beans; at times verity wasn't our strong suit. And I say 'ours' with extreme prejudice," she laughed, "because you know it's true. Did P.J. ever tell you about the time I dropped by but you weren't at home?"

He shook his head," No. When was this?"

"I didn't think he would. You and I were seeing each other, and it was right before our first major split. I was down in your neighborhood, coming back from Redondo, some shop to buy a blouse, and I stopped by your dad's. Don't even ask why, I know you didn't like me coming by and you were practically living in my house, but as I pulled by I saw the garage open in the back, and what a surprise, working on his car I saw P.J. I think P.J. and I had said like ten words to each other up to then, but I parked and walked back there and he was all 'Hey Nina, howza babe?' stuff. You weren't there, obviously, and he said you were at some bike parts store or something. I saw that Steve McQueen poster you had in there of him on your coveted T-6 from *The Great Escape,* and he noticed me looking. He started telling me McQueen raced bikes, and I informed him you had told me all that, and he went on that even Jimmy Dean had raced cars and bikes, and I figured out that since P.J. raced too, he was grouping himself in there as he leaned on his Fairlane. He offered me a beer and I declined, and then he asked if I thought he looked handsome! It was so weird and out of the blue. I mean, you resembled each other--- shared traits---but had distinctly different eyes and hair. His hair was coarser compared to yours and his eyes were darker, I recall. Your features finer and his thicker...you know what I mean. And he had started wearing his hair longish, but he still looked like a grease monkey. I told him he looked swell, and blah, blah Marty was a lucky woman, but he said to me in a real hushed tone as if she were in the kitchen, "Me and Marty are sort of on the outs. Have any girlfriends that look like you?" I almost laughed, thinking of Corinne. Anyway, at that point it started getting creepy as I didn't really know him and you never really talked about him too much other than to bitch about him when you would help him work on his car and sing *Maggie's Farm* substituting him as her brother. He started to flex his muscles; he was in a shirt with cut off sleeves, like another Kelleher I know, and he said he was stronger than you, and *bigger*. He was insinuating he had a bigger dick than you, and hey girl, come see about me. It was like some Bizarro-world moment out of *East of Eden* where the brothers were attracted to the same girl. It creeped me out to no end, so I left."

"He's dead, you know. Had a heart attack while he was driving. He was married to Marty too, and rest in peace probably her fucking cooking helped his heart implode. I didn't go to the funeral, and I never heard from her again. He and I were not very close for a long time. Since I moved to Hawaii. He and dad didn't even come to my wedding. That *is* a creepy story you just told. On the one hand I was like 'whoaaaa' and on the other I wanted to laugh at your predicament. I can't even remember him nude since we were little kids, so the dick mystery is just that. Marty and him were close forever…likes peas and carrots."

"Okay Forrest," she laughed, "how much farther is this place? I have to pee."

"We have miles to go…want more heat? It's freezing on this side of the Grapevine."

She looked out the blackened window into her own reflection, pulled back like a comic book impression on stretched silly putty, making her shiver to see it.

Chapter Forty-One

She was standing alone in the room, suitcase open, TV on but muted, and the entire room looking as if a scrum took place. The mini-bar was open from Tom rifling through it, and holding her clothes, she started dressing as if the room had caught fire. The room door would be wide open if it didn't have a pneumatic hinge as fast as he exited. She hooked her bra and swung it around her torso and pulled the cups up and went into her dress in a shimmy after adjusting her straps, which were fouled anyway. Into her shoes and making sure she had phone and purse, she started for the door, and then stopped at the open reefer door of the mini-bar. She saw some candy bars, a water, and three airline bottles of Absolut. She grabbed them all, water and a Twix and ran out of the room. She caught a glimpse of herself as she made it to the door and laughed at remembering the lines from *French Inhaler* and felt as if Death had brought her in a suitcase…grimly, she ran to the elevator and caught a car first hit.

In the lobby, she ran out of the door to see Tom just getting in the driver's side of his car, the sleepy valet taking some money from him and as he slowly pulled away, she caught him and pounded on the window. Stopping, he let her in. She looked at her hands and purse and wondered why she had grabbed the vodka. Habit? Desire?

Tom turned to her, feigning a yawn, "What took you?"

"Jesus, Tom...what the hell!"

They rode in silence as he drove east on Santa Monica Blvd. to the 405. Nina squibbed out a text, 'am o.k. Ttyl', sent it to Art, and then turned her phone off as the battery was low. Pure folly, she muttered to herself. She put the Absolut bottles in the console between driver and passenger, and rolled over on her side, exhausted.

As if Mary were next to him, Tom instinctively laid a hand on Nina's shoulder, unbuckled, and worming around placed his coat over her as he drove. Finding the entrance to the 405 North, he turned into it and started to Cholame.

Tom had measured most of his life in sections, chapters, and events. He would picture one era and know all about the contents...where he had been, things he had done. He slipped back into the days he and Nina had first started dating and saw himself as that boy, three years post mother's death and moving to their neighborhood in the South Bay. Nina lived off of Prospect where the houses looked fresh and sturdy, lawns well coiffed. Tom's dad bought a house east of there on the fringe of the school district where the tract homes built after the war for aeronautical and oil & gas workers started popping up.

When did he start to really remember things? Moving there was a blur, and even before, and without a picture he could barely remember his mother's face, like losing something over a boat into water, irretrievable and not even knowing where or when it was lost.

But Nina…it was as if when he met her he was kick-started. That section, chapter of his life seemed to always jump off his life's pages, his *beginning*. After teaching literature and humanities for over twenty-five years, he was convinced that certain things had meaning and thought of his life as a novel, uncompleted, and working its way to something. His planning to meet Nina, consummate his memories, and to do it selfishly, and carelessly didn't faze him. He admitted it was the closest thing to psychopathic behavior for him ever, even discounting his mad drunken bike travels to one house or another around the city to get laid when they had separated. He wasn't looking to leave Mary, but he also needed to figure out why he did it and what comes later. He likened it to an impulsive robbery in a bank when it was just a visit to make a deposit and turns into a hostage situation; unplanned and stupid, he didn't see a good ending. He was also starting to cough, and had to ask Nina not to smoke.

"You used to smoke those damn filter less coffin nails back in the day, boyo." she grudgingly stubbed out her cigarette and for one searing, frozen, and loud second, cracked a window and let it out of the car. "You know I almost bought a ticket to see you, when you moved to Oakland."

This surprised him, and also fed into the reservoir of ego he still held back by that mental dam where he kept her memories.

"Really?"

Nina tried to make out shapes in the dark as they drove through the valley, and then foothills to the Grapevine, but couldn't so stared out at the road bathed in the headlights as she tried to rekindle details from that time. "I can remember almost doing it, Tom, then forgetting why…like reading a headline, then forgetting the story underneath."

"Had I sent you that Dear Jane letter?"

"Yea, I think you had, and I was none too happy to get *that*! Look, it was always in *my* DNA to leave you, to change my mind, to abandon ship, but it was a slap of seriously cold water from you when you left, and the sick part of it was I was practically married to Cameron. Your '…even Abra forgave her father' shit…wow, I was pole-axed reading that. How stupid is that?"

So I wanted, I think, a reckoning with you, not so much as a hey baby, thinking of you, thing. I wanted to slap you or just rant. Underneath, I was hurt and felt stupid, and I was also mad at what a disaster it was when we reconnected. It made me realize we would probably never connect again like that."

Frowning, he remembered and didn't want to revisit it, but there it was, sitting next to him, and what better time to just bury it all than now? Hadn't Sheri said that exact thing, about this is the place to confess? Wasn't that why he was driving, almost into the dawn, to Cholame, to bury it all? "To be back with you then was good, but I also wanted to hurt you and didn't necessarily trust you anymore either. It was strange, in that I had these women stashed hither and yon, and was doing them when we were separated, but I continued. I wasn't man enough to tell you I was and made like I wasn't seeing them, but I was. It's the only way I can explain it. And we just imploded, not only from the deal with you wanting to live in Hollywood, but my being weak…first in seeing you again, then not being honest enough with you when we did hook up. I remember P.J. shaking his head, knowing you and I talked on the phone that night before I met you again at Gladstone's on Chautauqua, and as I walked out the door, he called after me 'p-whipped' and he was right. But like the song said, such an easy evil. I couldn't *not* see you, regardless of why or why not."

There was a silence in the car for a long stretch, then Nina said softly," There was a lot of the why or why not on both sides, Tom, so don't keep kicking yourself. So in the end, I just swallowed it, didn't spend the $60 bucks or whatever it was then to fly round trip to Oakland, and Cameron and I planned our wedding. I let that self that was part of you, us, just immerse itself until it was gone under the surface, and buried it deep. Like Marlowe, I lit a cigarette, had a cup of coffee, and said goodbye. Lame, but it worked. Until I dug you up and used you as a weapon against him. You came in handy, and I named my steely dan after you to further piss him off. I did a lot of things then that were very destructive, to myself and other people. I hurt my parents in a way that I still can't believe. Yea, they were stuffed shirts and sort of weird in their manifest destiny to make me an uber-daughter, but they loved me and I held them over the fire like a speared frog. They didn't deserve that."

"Are they still alive?"

"Yes, they live down in the South Bay still…sold their house and live in a nice little condo looking over King Harbor. You'll laugh, but when I was in the thick of it with Cameron, after I had come out of rehab that first time, my dad talked to me and he actually lamented you and I not marrying. Please, don't open the car door in your state of *non compos mentis* and hurl yourself out in space!" She laughed.

"Jesus! I'm too old for a fucking shock like that!" They both laughed.

Tom said in the silence afterward, "Rehab."

"Yes, one of many trips to the quiet room. I was a world class traveler there."

Chapter Forty-Two

She awoke with a start, and realized she had dozed off, her mouth feeling that sleep thickness in the corners, she took out some gum from her purse, quelling a desire to check her phone, figuring they were probably in a dead zone way out wherever they were.

Nina turned to him, feeling catholic in their small bubble of the car. "Remember that night I called you from the restaurant, and you rode out?"

He smiled in the dark, "I do."

"I always felt when we reconnected that night, we were like the Divers in *Tender is the Night,* bound together by this huge secret we both shared, but unlike them, from our growing up together, not an affliction, and we also shared this strong spiritual link in what we created. That no matter the malady, we were immune having shared so much, yet it wasn't enough because even together we didn't make that whole, and like Dick, you strayed and like Nicole, I looked for an exit all the time, knowing what we had was seriously broken even in loving you. Pushing the apartment search in Hollywood was my way of generating that exit, like I knew you wouldn't bite off on it, and as much as I loved you, had invested in you, was inside you---and you,

I---it wasn't going to happen. And you *didn't* bite, and we separated to the point you planned your exit. Like Nicole, I found my mercenary, my jump-off and even though he proved to be a piece of shit, he was there and we talked the same bullshit, shared the same experiences, you didn't subscribe to that bullshit and pursued your vision. Like Dick, you geographically disappeared, as if you could only breath normally with me far away, not tempting you. But also, Tommy, you were stronger than Dick. You didn't disappear into the ether and start weakening, you had that weird Conradian twist in you...the being able to do things on your own and just *go.* Even though you didn't speak my language by then, you spoke one I couldn't. You spoke independence, and unlike me, able to be by you, live by yourself. I was always, even though I would never admit it, like a trapeze artist swinging from one seat to another needing that security of the swing and a partner with outstretched arms. Yes, I would be suspended in mid-air to the gasp of the audience---caught in space alone for that brief second---but never self-reliant to the point of making that leap alone. I swung from you to Cameron, and made my Faustian choice in whom I let catch me, but you could Tom, and you did, and I always secretly admired you as you went that a way, sailing into the sunset and not minding me. We just split and it was never meant to be. The sex? Yea...still there obviously, but also so for dogs and raccoons, we'll never lose that and I won't ever forget this part of it, but it was never enough to sustain anything. After I met Art, I realized how much I needed stability and not chaos. I thought that made me or gave me *character*, me---he's older and had also been over the coals in his first marriage and it's weird because as much damage as I inflicted on him, far more than his first wife, he never wavered; he stood fast for me and I had to respect that more than anything. It touched me deeper than anything I had ever experienced. Yea, you and I shared that magical first court and spark that is the never get it again sort of stuff, but it doesn't have staying power; like youth withers on us in time. The love I have for Art has that staying power, and it's learned. You earn it like hard fought winnings in life every day, as your mate either measures up or out. It's so weird how you still excite me and ignite all those girlhood memories, and a slew of what-ifs and you're forever in my sky. You're always up there, shining to the direction of those things, but like tonight, it just isn't real. Was it our immaturity or were we always just a volatile and toxic cocktail when we mixed...I don't know, but we both needed someone different to make our lives work."

"A lot of what-ifs," Tom said softly. They were almost at Blackwell's Corner and the Texaco station there. They both needed the facilities and to gas up. "For me, if I heard a certain song, or saw a woman with thick blonde hair, or wearing Shalimar walked by, I immediately thought of you, and be back there. I had no sway over it, no control at all. I would weaken, like I always did; it was the thread that ran through me, the string that held my entire being together. I was rigged that way. My inability to be honest with you, in case of tipping the applecart, even when I knew you weren't faithful to me. I'd sit and ask myself, why is that, Tom? I'd never answer myself, just shrug it off, ride to some woman's house, and fuck it off. But you were always the green light at the end of the dock."

◐◐◐

"I killed my first baby." It was just audible over the music, opening Tom's ears as a result.

He was looking at the road, a thin line of light in the gloom, the mountain to the side, and ahead blank, in hiding. They crossed the summit for the road and were in descent. Moving his jaws, working his ears, popping in-between her words. Eastward, dawn was fast approaching.

"I was married happily to Art a couple of years and was out of rehab and sober a long time. But I just couldn't, for some reason, wrap myself around the baby thing, and especially when I didn't trust myself half the time. I snapped. Every fear I had was alive on the surface of my skin like I was immersed in this piercing, crawling dread. I didn't deserve the happiness, I didn't deserve the honor --- all that. And I saw this vision of failing, miserably, and Art finally seeing me this way as if I had been a hoax --- just this dummy someone had been throwing a voice into for ages and I cringed. I failed. I went right out and bought booze at a Thrifty's of all places! After that I took a powder and fucked I don't know who or what. I was found and hospitalized and I had lost my baby. I had induced myself by drinking…stuffing myself with booze and I think someone hopped me up and also stuffed a few pricks into me ---junk and men in---baby out. I can still see Art's face when I finally came out of it and was clear, realized it *was* him. I had seen him before when I was out of my mind, a bad memory like that over the top *Dr. Jekyll and Mr. Hyde* with Jack Palance…yes, I am pulling that one out of my hat…all I could think of when I saw him and I was hopped up was Palance's leering face saying "Looking for Mr. Hyde, were you?" I was Hyde. When I finally did become cognizant and saw his beautiful baldhead and those eyes of his, I felt as if I were saved like a river baptism in a John Ford movie saved; Ward Bond dunking me under. You know I never believed in all that, but in his eyes it was so, that I was breathing and had returned from this baptism in destruction."

"The baby issue never came up, ever. Not a word. I saw it in his eyes. No one ever looked at me that way, Tom. You and I never went there. And so I resolved that I'd make a perfect baby with him. And if boy, Alexander, and if a girl, Alexandria ---conquerors to vanquish in me all I had been. And I had a beautiful boy. See what a good show you missed?" She had a small soft laugh to herself.

Tom held the wheel listening to her and even as her words faded into her question, he tried to see Nina that way. As her story held up images to him, it was hard to see it. It took him some ugly directions to see her that way.

"Did I frighten you?" Her voice was calm, thinking now of Art. "All of that and here I am in a car, coming down a mountain with my first lover. The man whose vodka lips made me implode. The lover who still, after almost forty years knows my old body and still finds those places that makes me cry. Pure folly, aren't we? Sorry, this is stuff I should've kept a lid on. I'm here because I wanted to be here and that's that. I keep forgetting how I planned this, dressed for this, and wanted to open my legs for this, and now just feel like that strung out cunt from yesteryear." She was dying for a cigarette in the closed car; *the hall of mirrors* she laughed inside, seeing her reflection in every glass surface.

Clearing his throat to make sure he didn't allow a word to frog or squawk, now he attempted to speak but then didn't. They were descending faster and he pictured the flattened valley out before them from the past, riding down the Grapevine with his dad and P.J. as kids, onto old 99 enroute to Fresno to see some long lost uncle who had become a Jehovah's Witness. After a few miles he spoke.

"You don't frighten me, just hard to see you that way with what I have to remember you by."

"When I was married to Cameron, I finally became who I had always been, always knew what was inside me. Not very nice, eh? I was a total candidate for a snake pit...thought I would end up like old Sophie, throat slashed and fished out of some harbor," she said matter of factly.

"I remember when you gave me *Razor's Edge*. It was one of those life-changing reads."

"Yea...and you wanted to become Larry Darrell."

Nina laughed at him softly.

"So this *is* the confessional hour? When I danced with Sheri last night? She said she had a crush on me back in the day. I almost died of shock."

Nina pulled her lips out, duckbilled, "Sure it is. Sheri, huh? Can't imagine her, Ms. Student Body and you lasting a night. Go ahead, if you can beat my drunken tramp period."

"I have mesothelioma."

She looked out the window again; knowing all she would see was an elasticated reflection. "You sure know how to steal a scene, Tom. When did all this happen, from your shipyard, sailor days?"

"Yes. Pulling down lagging from the overheads on the ships wrapped around the piping, machinery. So yea…all asbestos," He laughed. "Not very romantic."

"Are you being treated…are you taking anything?" She was not wishing to, but already thinking of him now as *gone*. Tom dead. It made her shiver. For her, it was also a selfish 'there but for the grace of God' go I, moment. She didn't need that *affliction* yet!

Regardless of telling her, he still held this image of Nina as she described her ordeal of relapse. He couldn't believe that person held next to his ideal memory of her. It *did* frighten him, more than he realized. He knew she could be cold at times, even verbally destructive, but to hear of her as a full-blown drinker and addict was beyond him. He didn't want to surrender that memory, the one he had fleshed out when needing to cut the rope, or to make no apologies for. That was a woman who had artistic *temperament* and not suicidal urges.

"Tom…are you taking any treatments? Chemo or radiation, or whatever they do?"

"I haven't really started. I just found out right before we started communicating. Mary doesn't know."

She was struck by his words, "Tom, why in the fuck wouldn't you start or tell?"

He didn't know if he could articulate it, as he had had the

conversation in his head since learning of it. He couldn't explain his dangerous game of balance knowing he was absolutely mortal and had the power to decide to live or die. That immortality he embraced when younger when that Triumph had become his rocket ship, his fighter plane, had started to fall away as he aged. The fearless vision he had shed in time like his skin fading back to white in the winter. Daily, he became more mortal and it was even harder recalling that feeling. But now, in his defiance, he felt some vigor and bravado, and his balls. He held that feeling in his hands and it gave him the rush he used to have when opening the bike throttle wide open on PCH.

In the Dead Time, he had embarked on a trip down to Cardiff-by-the-Sea to visit a woman he had chanced to meet in Venice Beach. She had been at the Boardwalk bookstore sipping coffee in the outdoor café. Tom noticed the book she was reading before he really took her in. She had Miller's *Air Conditioned Nightmare* in front of her face and he just stopped and took a seat across from her. Women and books. Nina had surely spoiled him and he fancied himself an intellectual hick surrounded by intelligent women. His flame of attraction. After a few cups of coffee and half a pack of her cigarettes, they made a date for him to visit her in Cardiff, since she was visiting and at her sisters in L.A. and couldn't see him there because her time was limited. So, the next weekend he strapped a small ditty bag with a bungee on the small rack he had fitted onto the back of the saddle seat and fender of the Thunderbird filled with sundries in the event of an overnighter or a hotel visit and off he went south.

His ride was without incident until he hit the stretch of I-5 after

San Clemente and Trestles. Some surfers sitting their boards, others riding lazy waves, and the nuclear plant at San Onofre, like two giant teats jutting up, were still gray and depressing. As the hills of the Marine base rose up at Las Pulgas and Basilone Roads and with the Pacific to his right, Tom opened the throttle as wide as it could go and with the twin pipes thumping, he shot through the air on this dead calm day, a landlocked meteorite. He felt something he never had before…he knew he was transcendent as his speed picked up, and he experienced a calm and a peace he never knew as he passed cars easily, but seeing details of each one even as he was himself a blur. He became what he imagined was some state of invisibility and cloaked that way, immortal in that moment.

When he came out of the other side of Pendleton into Oceanside, it were as if he awoke from a trance slowly, like Icarus, pin wheeling back to earth as Tom himself reentered his body again mortal and plain. For some reason he recalled what he had read were Dean's last words to his mechanic, seated next to him, "That guy has to see us."

He barely remembered exiting past Encinitas to find her place. He spent a relatively pleasant but boring evening browsing her expansive library, drinking some good Chardonnay, and feigning interest in her divorce and settlement. The sex, while good, was just for him going through motions, and he floated above it, a somnambulist still in the thrall of those seventeen miles of highway. The absolute control over his life, the feel of the wind and in between the brown hills of Pendleton and the stark blue of the sea, he cut through both on that border of road in between them. Even between his hostess's legs it was all he felt and thought of, and so it was now, sitting on the precipice of his condition, treatment, and mortality.

Turning his head to Nina he couldn't find the words to explain it, and just drove, feeling in her silence a growing contempt for the situation he could recognize from when they were young and together.

◯◯◯

It was quiet again between them, Tom sensing that after each spoke; the pauses became more pregnant, heavier. When they spoke it was as if they were dancing slowly, holding each other apart slightly, not wishing to step on each other's feet. They moved gingerly, to a strange uneven rhythm they weren't familiar with and had not practiced for. Neither had even really thought they would play out this end of their relationship; only living in the memory of it, so the nuance of conversation was foreign and unscripted.

He thought to himself about when they were together, he and Nina, and had admitted that back then it wasn't near any state of nirvana, and every day was a challenge for them. He felt it was a stable relationship at the time, yet was a part of a fragmentation of many others, as if he were leading seriously different lives at once and none being more or less than the other…dependent on what happened, and in some cases it wasn't pretty. He recalled his slap across the face, and confronting the truth of his sick need for Celeste. Nina and he, while feeling on firm ground, were very jaggedly fragile – attempting to construct something on an untenable foundation, and now to seize a piece of the past which totally contravenes their current situations. Just way too much has transpired in the years that have passed, at the crucible, they each failed in their own ways to have the courage and strength to stand together and weather their storms, and now it's too late for anything but a trip to an ancient car wreck site! A pilgrimage to death and chaos, and he had to smile at it.

Chapter Forty-Three

There was the creeping of day, and above him, the pink mackerel sky dissipating and giving way to blue, the clouds beautiful in their patterns. It sent a chill up him in his suit pants, pumping gas at the Texaco at Lost Hills. There was the back of the James Dean square puzzle sign of his head…looked like from *Rebel*. Tom started at the back of it, as he finished pumping, his fingers freezing on the pump handle.

Nina got out wearing his coat against the cold, and had gone to use the facility…her words from the car filled him in the chill of post sunrise. He imagined Mary looking at him now, and he felt foolish and silly, coughing more, and knowing full well she'd be shaking her head, admonishing him in that simple "What're you doing, haole-boy?" look. He felt silly as he stood looking over the bleak ribbon of road stretching west, visible only in places, like the back of a swimming snake in the greyish light. He looked over and saw Nina smoking a cigarette, waving as he walked over to the Dean picture on posts. Jimmy's big head looked wistfully away into the morning, offering nothing. There was also a tall full body poster cut-away of Dean from *Rebel*, Tom's favorite Dean movie, with his red collar up, that turned up bow of his mouth in that amused smile he always seemed to have. She came back to the car.

"Weird to think he gassed up here the last time…well, not here exactly but the station that was here in the day. Inside, they have this creepy mannequin sitting in there that's supposed to be him. It looked like a man-sized Jerry Mahoney!" They laughed at the lewd image of Mahoney as Dean, but at the same time were pulling away from each other.

◯◯◯

As they drove out from Lost Hills, his mood shifted to a darker place. Like a sickness, it started slowly and then spread into all of his being, leaving its trail inside him. He kept his own counsel, and like in the past, when Nina told him something he just absorbed it and internalized, letting it take its course unheeded. She described her going off the rails and in her words, "killing her baby", when her fears overcame her reason. It was hard to see Nina as that person. He had never known her to harbor any fears, so the thought of it was alarming to him, as if he discovered one of his idols had been discovered to have a side that was unsavory and disturbing. He just never entertained anything about her in that way, and remembering her story, it made him feel weakened inside. It reminded him of the selfishness of his hiding his own real illness from Mary, and why he had. It was unnerving to him to think Nina had that weakness as well. Her actions, when described, pulling back the curtain on his own vision of Oz, had gut-punched him.

In the car, there seemed to be a wall between them, ethereal and full of past ghosts neither knew about. The memories he had when getting his car out of the garage at the hotel were distant, unreal, and in light of her revelations, pure folly. Ahead was what? What did it mean? He reached into the console, took out one of the small Absolut bottles, and started twisting the cap.

"Little early for that isn't it...or are we that way?"

He laughed softly, "Not really that way, but now it is."

"You're thinking of what I told you...when I went off and lost my kid, cuckolded Art, and smoked up a barn of shit. You're astonished and outraged, and like watching a spider or a cobra, fascinated and repelled simultaneously...yes, no?"

"Yes, no." The silence that followed was punctuated only by the low strains of the iPod music from Tom's machine. He took note of the incongruity of listening to the Surf Riders as they spoke, and what memories that evoked. He had a quick vision of he and Mary with their boards at Maka Pu'u and feeling the heat from the sand burning into his back after lying down exhausted, then looking out at the barren brown rollers of hills, like static muddy waves, surrounding him. The vodka burned smoothly into him, spreading like a fluid fire in him.

"I did some foolish things, things I never imagined. I would hold my past up to what I was doing in the present...do you understand that? And as I did, my shame would multiply, and my self-loathing stock skyrocketed...remembering things...like just playing guitar in my room alone, listening to the strings as I played, and the sound. Then I was smoking some hop and waking up in some weird bed in Compton, in some shotgun shack in Pomona, not knowing where my underwear was…my husband at home schizzing out. My rentals wringing their hands for my *King's Row* melodramatic psychodramas." She turned to look out the window.

I guess I'm doing that now, he said inside, scared to utter it, his Nina default. It was hard to see her that way, disheveled, incoherent, cringing, and worst of all in fear. He had never given any thought to her husband, Art, but in that moment, he respected his resolve and love for Nina. He was embarrassed in that same instance at what Mary had for him, and how he had corkscrewed it.

Route 46, as it was called now, connected like a small artery to the main road at 101, linking it to I-5 in the east. The closest Tom had ever come to it was riding north on 101 and stopping in Paso Robles to piss. By the time he drove past the connection to Cholame, the need or memory to do it had been buried post Nina. He was on his way north to Oakland and having shipped whatever clothes and books he needed, enjoyed a long and leisurely ride up north. He hadn't realized he was just twenty-five miles from his destination then. Now they navigated the Polonio Pass, dropping into the valley, rolling easily on the road. Tom took off his glasses, now that day was underway and the road ahead was undemanding and flowed out in front of them. He leaned over to the dashboard and dropping the glove box, extracted his sunglasses.

Nina smiled, but didn't wish to make eye contact. "You still wear those, after all these years," she stated matter of factly.

"Yes, one thing I could never give up…and anyway, JFK was

right about a few things." Their voices held no emotion, like an empty vessel they had drained, now empty and hollow. The lovemaking post reunion, when they had made their escape almost forgotten. The road itself seemed void of any emotion as well. Dunn colored hills, and the two-lane blacktop punctuated by yellow lines, lazy, and rolling as they drove Dean's last miles. The sky looking out to the west, the Pacific had lightened and was a cheerful, yet bland blue, a shade darker than its skin to the east.

Nina hated the silence, wondered what she could say to break it, worried about the ride home…the next three hours after this adventure terminated, back to Los Angeles. She missed Art, had already, she knew, hurt him deeply. She was running damage control in her head, picturing herself at a landline talking to Corinne and then constructing her story for Art, wondering how much of it would include the truth. Jesus, she thought, I am fucking fifty-eight, and here I am still concocting junior high stories to save my skin. She attempted to turn her anger on Tom, then as fast as that feeling rose, it dissipated quickly, like windblown smoke. She had come along, she had answered his e-mail, she had corresponded and wanted to see him, dressed for him wishing to arouse him…so what fault his?

"On your Facebook page, that bike you're working on, I never asked you what it was."

He pictured it on his work stand, surrounded by all the tools that gave him such security, "It's a Triumph Trident. 750 ccs. Almost done, too."

"For some reason I remember you always wanting to rebuild

an old Norton Commando."

"I did…but too hard to find parts." Like it's too hard to find words now, he mused. There was a forced tone to the words they shared now. There wasn't anger, just nothing.

"Does your wife ride?"

"She did, always on back. When we were younger and just met, I shipped our…*my* bike to Hawaii and we rode everywhere…it was all I had, and her car was junk, and always breaking down. It was an Island beater she bought down near the base on Nimitz, lots of cheap car dealerships for sailors, from money she earned when young." Tom felt better talking about her, something that didn't take an effort or have to be worked at. "She used to model as a kid, local stuff there, wearing island clothes, and leis. She used most for her tuition to school, so she wouldn't have to take out loans or ask her parents for anything."

"She sounds very noble and also very focused."

Tom laughed, "And yet she still married me! But I started to focus then too, and decided to go into teaching. Did you ever think I would?"

She thought of that, of his nature, always giving to her when he could, always studying things, and decided it wasn't such a stretch. "I can see it." When younger, she wondered for him, where would he go, what would he do? Her father would snort that if she wanted to see him at work, she'd have to start riding a bike that broke down, sentencing him to the gulag of a repair shop. Nina would shudder thinking of him coming home, smelling of bike engines, and cigarettes.

"When did you quit smoking?"

"The day I met Mary, and she told me kissing smokers was like licking an ashtray. I tossed my cigarettes that night. I suppose I'm just a mat for what women want," he laughed.

Nina laughed, "Didn't stop you from kissing me."

"No," he said in a smaller voice, "it didn't. But it was you."

"You're not a mat, Tom. You're just different. You never told me, "You can't do that", and never was critical or had an 'I told you so' in your heart. You may feel as if you were riding pillion in life with me, but I just felt equal to you, and that's really how it should be, isn't it? You walked the walk as a man. I never felt competitive or in a race with you. I always felt that if I looked to the side, you were there and that was a good thing for a woman growing up in our time. You attract women with that, and I know your wife saw it as well. So don't sell your stocks short, boyo" She was tired now, and looking at the roadside asked, "Are we almost there?"

"Yes, I believe so."

They sighted the Jack Ranch Café and the tree. It was called the Tree of Heaven and was embraced by a stainless steel and concrete box with large letters and numerals in relief, unlike a gravestone with the words and dates cut into it. The café was closed and they huddled in the car, staring at the tree.

Tom opened his door and pulled himself out by the frame, and walked to it. It read:

JAMES DEAN
1931 Feb 08 1955 Sep 30 PM 5:59 ∞

He sat, the sun reflecting off the metal of the memorial. The spring sun was higher, the clouds that were outlined in fading crimson and pink were scattered now and trailing east away from the valley they were in. Tom looked out over the road. He imagined that last September day and how warm it must have been, Dean still in his tee shirt, the heat of the day still lingering as the sun dipped lower to the tops of the hills that rolled like ceaseless breakers to the coast from the road Dean died on.

The '8' from his birthdate and the '19' from his death year date were missing. Tom stared at it for a few moments and then touched the letters and numerals, stopping on the sign for infinity. It felt smooth and reptilian under his fingers, silver and brisk.
Nina quietly come up next to him, wrapping his coat around her close. "Creepy isn't it?"

Tom brought his fingertips down from the infinity symbol, rubbing them together, feeling the dust. "Yea." Looking out the road to the west, he saw a semi-truck moving towards them at a high speed. There was a bench and he sat, and she sat next to him but apart. She pulled a cigarette out and turning her back to the small breeze, she lit it. Exhaling, she turned to him, smiling.

"Do you remember that first time we kissed? How fluid it was? You were the first boy I ever kissed and it was the most natural thing ever. I remember thinking you would kiss me forever Tom, and we would grow old and make babies…all of it. This beautiful vision like in the movies." She paused and dragged on her cigarette. "You tasted like almonds that first night and it was wonderful and every man who ever kissed me after you had to meet that threshold, rise to *your* lips. Some of them I enjoyed sexually of course, but couldn't bring myself to kiss them, failing miserable to make that cut for me."

Tom had almost always denied Celeste his mouth, not wishing to give her that, preferring her in a position where the intimacy of his lips could be excused away.

"Even my first husband---could never be you as a lover. It was convenient; we were in the same racket and at the time *wasn't you.* I was so passive-aggressive then and anyway, we were immolating…but that first time at the movies---you spoiled my mouth, and the feel of your hair, that silkiness in my fingers almost like holding water…does that make sense? I never forgot that. And then when we kissed in the cab last night that was the first time in years I had tasted alcohol ---that and your lips made it feel as if a landmine had gone off in my head. Your kiss felt the same as it did that night we were fourteen. But…I can close the book on it. On you. I'm not angry…I don't say this harshly, Tom. I just know after this it is over. I should have cut that rope ages ago, yet couldn't so I want to tell you things now. Thank you for what you made me feel, the experiences we shared. It was beautiful, but it was then, and that's that. But I can't have, at this time of my life, my skeletons all throwing a party for me and engaging in more damages or grotesque moments of flight," she said it softly, but with a certain finality he couldn't mistake, knowing when she meant things and when she did not.

Tom looked up at the missing '8' and wondered what wall it adorned and where? Europe? Local? Or was it taken in some moment of caprice and relegated to the garage or a trunk in an attic. He wondered if it were taken in lieu of the infinity symbol and rests on its side. He looked at her through his sunglasses. Well, at least she is true to herself. How could he forget her?

Chapter Forty-Four

A green sedan pulled up quietly and four younger people, two men, and two women alighted. All were Japanese. All wore skinny jeans, multi-colored high tops and motorcycle jackets. The men had longish hair swept up into elaborate Jett Rink pompadours that were died a bright yellow blonde, as were the women, who both wore red NY Yankee ball caps on backwards. They all had sleek and small Oakley's hiding their eyes. They walked to the Tree.

"Ahh … Seita Onishi," the tall man, the driver, said elaborately.

"*Hai.*" The other three answered, dropping their heads in a small bowing motion. They all came to stand in front of Tom and Nina, admiring the tree and the inscription. Tom took them in and smiled at their dress. Nina smoked and had turned away, disinterested. The tall one, the driver, turned to Tom.

"This is art by a Japanese…Seita Onishi." Pointing at the stainless cage, his accent not so thick. "We arso rike James Dean." He smiled. Then waving his own fingers, circling them above his painted hair, pointed with his other hand to Tom's flowing white locks, "Ha! You old James Dean!" The others gave Tom the same head motions as they listened to the driver speak to him. "Now we go to the shrine at the junction. You know where?"

Tom knew it was just west and told them sure, to follow him. He held his hand out for Nina and taking it, she followed him back to the car. They drove silently up to the roadside where a bland green State sign read: James Dean Memorial Junction, where the two roads met, and where they adjoined, Dean had slipped into infinity...Dean, caught in time forever as that younger man. Tom held that image of him in his mind a second and then saw himself forever immortalized for that moment on the road, on his Thunderbird, in that spiritual moment of high speed.

Nina stood at the wire fence to the side of the road, and looked to the north, on her phone out of earshot from Tom. The Japanese couples that had followed them up were taking pictures of each other, talking animatedly and smoking, aping for the pictures by throwing shakas and ersatz gang signs. They reminded Tom of his students, and he smiled inwardly.

Nina put her phone away and was talking to the tall driver, who had good English and he nodded as she talked, and looked over at Tom. Nina then walked to Tom as he leaned on the memorial junction sign.

"I'm going with them. They're headed up onto I-5 and will take me to Bakersfield where I can grab a plane south. I...I just can't see driving back together now. Can you?" She chuckled a bit. "I told them we were desperadoes, and they bought into it. They dug that idea."

Tom nodded and silently took back his coat, the Shalimar a faint scent on the morning breeze as he stooped and kissed her cheek. He rolled it around his arm and leaned again on the sign pole. Tom wondered if he resembled a skeleton as he watched them, shaking it off.

They all got into the sedan, Nina in between the two girls in the back. Tom watched from the memorial sign as Nina took out a hand mirror, her lips pouting as she surveyed the damage of last night, the heavy bell of her blonde hair radiant and amazing in its fullness in comparison to the two peroxided and lank haired girls on either side. They needed to negotiate a U-Turn to return to I-5 and head to Bakersfield. The car pulled alongside Tom and started to turn, thinking he saw a glance from Nina, or hoped he had, but then knew he hadn't.

One of the Japanese girls threw him a peace sign, he returned it, and then the car was going in the opposite direction. As it became smaller, he looked above it to the high rolling hills of the Polonio Pass; from where he stood, the old road from 1955, a faded, overgrown two-lane tattoo almost ethereal on the golden slopes just a few hundred yards from the new road. Everything had shifted since those days and the road he stood on itself was altered and renamed numerically. The past. Standing in it, looking at it, living in it. She was right. The past, where he looked at the now tiny green car, disappeared for him.

Tom felt stronger now as the air warmed and he didn't feel like coughing. He'd fly home, start treatment, and spend a long time laying next to Mary and tell her things. He ran his hand through his hair, and then it was gently pushed to one side by a small breeze. No reason to ever consider again swimming against the current of time. He had nothing before him but the stretch of future, much like the Polonio, curving through the landscape. Another car pulled up and a young couple got out smiling at him and started snapping pictures of the sign and themselves.

"Excuse me, mister?" The younger man asked, Tom, "Can you take our picture together? We've talked about nothing but coming here since we saw *East of Eden* at a film festival during Christmas!"

Tom took their cell phone and telling them to smile, snapped a couple of pictures. He gave them back the phone and as they thanked him, he pulled out his own phone and asked them for a picture of him as well. He stood next to the sign and did his best Jimmy face from memory. Taking back his phone, he looked back toward Polonio Pass and saw that the green car had disappeared from sight.

End

About the Author

Raised in California, Doc Krinberg held myriad jobs to include taxi driver, strip club barker and truck driver for a junkyard before a career as a navy hardhat diver and journeyman academic. The good Doctor divides his time between helping raise his three sons, admiring his daughter's dancing skills, supporting his wife's career as a naval officer and instructing doctoral courses in educational leadership.

He is a published poet, loves his choc lab Jack, Harley Davidson Motorcyles, and hopes that the Raiders return to their former glory.

<u>Aignos Publishing, Inc.</u>

Aignos (pronounced "I-Know" from a German word meaning "Confederates bound by oath") Publishing is an independent, bilingual royalty-based publisher. We specialize in experimental and inventive fiction and nonfiction works. We seek bold, boundary-pushing works from today's most exciting authors.

If you liked Doc Krinberg's book, then please check out our other wonderful Aignos titles at www.aignos.com:

Lawyers Gone Bad, Vincent Scarsella
An Aura of Greatness, Brendan P. Burns
El Camino de Regreso, Maricruz Acuna
Letters, Buz Sawyers
In Conversation, Chris Campanioni
Going Down, Chris Campanioni
Feast of Saint Sebastian, Jon Marcantoni
Nuno, Carlos Aleman
Happy That It's Not True, Carlos Aleman
University and King, Jeffery Ryan Long
John Doe, Buz Sawyers
Anonymous Man, Vincent Scarsella
There's No Cholera in Zimbabwe, Zachary Oliver & Jon Marcantoni
When Angels Fall, Manuel Melendez
Overnight Family Man, Paul Guzzo
Piano Tuner's Wife, Jean Yamasaki Toyama
Covering the Sun with my Hand, Theresa Varela
Dark Side of Sunshine, Paul Guzzo
The Desert and the City, Derek Bickerton

www.ingramcontent.com/pod-product-compliance
Lightning Source LLC
Chambersburg PA
CBHW070755280626
47162CB00016B/898